HD · MW

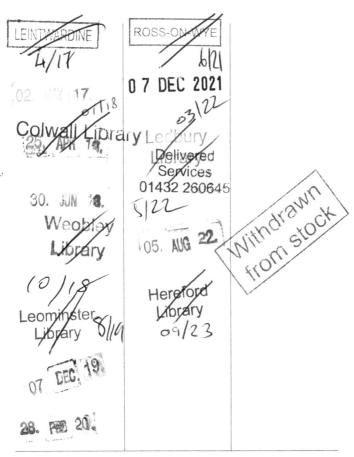
Please return/renew this item by the last date shown

**Herefordshire
Libraries**

*Herefordshire
Council*

Stranded in His Arms

Falling in love in the face of danger!

As the water level rises in a Somerset village ambulance partners Mimi Sawyer and Jack Halliday race towards a pregnant woman fast approaching her due date. But when a river bursts its banks this fearless team is separated, and Mimi and Jack find themselves facing the strongest challenge yet to the walls around their hearts…!

Don't miss this exciting new duet by

Annie Claydon

Mimi and Rafe's story
Rescued by Dr Rafe

and

Jack and Cass's story
Saved by the Single Dad

Available now!

Dear Reader,

I've often thought that to read—and write—romance you have to be a believer in redemption. Is it *really* possible to leave the past behind and make a new future? Mimi and Rafe have a tough task on their hands, because they've hurt each other before and have spent the last five years rebuilding their lives. The last thing either of them wants to do is go back and revisit that pain. So working together for even a few days, in a flood-ravaged area, is a particular challenge for them.

But sometimes tough times will give us the chance of a new beginning. Looking back on my own life, I can see the many good times have given me joy and hope, but it's the difficult times which have shaped me the most and given me the opportunity to change. And, of course, to appreciate those good times all the more!

Thank you for reading Rafe and Mimi's story. I always enjoy hearing from readers, and you can contact me via my website at annieclaydon.com.

Annie x

RESCUED BY
DR RAFE

BY
ANNIE CLAYDON

MILLS
BOON®

First published in Great Britain 2016
By Mills & Boon, an imprint of HarperCollins*Publishers*
1 London Bridge Street, London, SE1 9GF

Large Print edition 2017

© 2016 Annie Claydon

ISBN: 978-0-263-06685-2

Printed and bound in Great Britain
by CPI Antony Rowe, Chippenham, Wiltshire

Cursed with a poor sense of direction and a propensity to read, **Annie Claydon** spent much of her childhood lost in books. A degree in English Literature followed by a career in computing didn't lead directly to her perfect job—writing romance for Mills & Boon—but she has no regrets in taking the scenic route. She lives in London: a city where getting lost can be a joy.

Books by Annie Claydon

Mills & Boon Medical Romance

Visit the Author Profile page at millsandboon.co.uk for more titles.

For my sweet sister

CHAPTER ONE

THE RAIN BEAT down hard on the windscreen, the wipers only clearing it for a moment before water blocked visibility again. Jack was sitting next to her, watching the road ahead carefully.

'Think we'll make it?'

Mimi was gripping the steering wheel tight, gauging the way the heavy vehicle was responding in the wet conditions. 'Yep. As long as the road doesn't disappear out from under us, we'll make it.'

The comment wasn't as unlikely as it would have sounded when they'd last come this way, two weeks ago. It had been raining then, a fine mist that barely covered the road ahead of them. But since then, the rain hadn't stopped. It had been a dismal summer and August had brought storms. Roads had been washed away in some areas of rural Somerset, and ambulance crews had been battling to get through to their patients.

'Just think. In two weeks' time you'll be away from all of this.' Jack leaned back in his seat. 'Miss Miriam Sawyer. Paramedic.'

Despite herself, Mimi grinned. She'd worked hard, and the sound of her own name, spoken with the coveted qualification attached still made her smile every time Jack repeated it. 'I'm not sure I would have made it without you.'

''Course you would. Although I like to think that my expertise and advice were helpful...'

'And the incessant nagging, of course. But we don't mention that.'

'No, we don't. Or my back seat driving.'

'Especially not that.' Two weeks seemed like a long time right now and Mimi's promotion from ambulance driver to paramedic a long way away. Just getting to this call was about as far ahead as she was able to think, right now.

'And I'll be trying to get used to a new partner. Missing your unerring instinct for finding every bump in the road...'

'Oh, put a sock in it.' Mimi felt her shoulders relax. Jack always knew when the tension was getting too much, and always seemed to be able to wind things down a bit. 'Anyway, you're assuming that they'll be able to find someone who'll put up with you.'

'Harsh, Mimi. Very harsh.' Jack chuckled, leaning forward to see ahead of them, down the hill towards the river. 'Looks as if the bridge is still there.'

'Yeah, but I don't think we should risk it. That bridge will only just take an ambulance at the best of times. I don't want to get stuck in the mud on the other side.' In the brief moments that the windscreen was clear enough to see any distance, it was apparent that the surface water, rolling down the hill on the far side of the river, had reduced the road to a slippery quagmire.

Jack nodded. 'Looks as if we walk the rest of the way, then.'

'We could try the A389.' They'd been directed around this way because of reports that the main road into the village was closed. But maybe that was just a precaution and the ambulance would still be able to traverse it.

'Nah, I checked and it's under three feet of water. We'd never get through.' Jack had been using his phone for updates while Mimi concentrated on the driving. 'Right now, I think we need to just get ourselves there.'

'And then?' If the chances of getting the ambulance across the bridge and up to the village at the top of the hill on the other side were slim, the thought of arriving on foot didn't appeal very much either. Bringing a pregnant woman back down that treacherous path was something that didn't bear thinking about.

'We can assess the situation. I've put a call in for a doctor to attend…'

'Yeah. Right.' She and Jack had delivered babies before together and, if needs must, they'd do it again. 'I hope they're not going to send some junior doctor who thinks he's the one who's going to save the world and that we should just stand back and make the tea.'

'As a paramedic you'll be making these kinds of decisions soon. What will you do?' Jack smiled.

'Oh, I think I'll put in a call for a doctor to attend.' Mimi grinned back at him, bringing the ambulance to a halt. She decided to stay put and not pull off the road on to the muddy verge. That was one sure way to get stuck, and a car could make it past in the other lane. Anything bigger wouldn't be getting any further anyway.

'Time to get your hair wet again.'

Mimi grimaced, tucking her blonde plait into the back of her shirt. Her hair had been wet so many times in the last week that she was beginning to wish that short hair suited her as well as it did Jack.

They pulled their wet weather gear on in the cabin and Mimi reached for the radio. The only response to her call signal was a burst of static. 'Looks as if there's a problem again...'

'Yeah?' Jack looked at the rain slamming into the windscreen. 'Have you got a signal on your mobile?'

'Probably not...' Even in good conditions, mobile reception was patchy around here. 'I might have to walk back up the road a bit. You go on; I'll be right behind you.'

The ambulance rocked slightly as Jack pulled his heavy bag out of the back, slamming the rear doors closed. Mimi saw him trudge past, rain bouncing from his waterproofs, as she pulled out her phone and dialled.

Nearly... A staccato ringtone sounded on the

line, but it was breaking up and then it cut out completely. Climbing out of the ambulance, she toiled back along the road, rain stinging her face. Some way ahead of her she could see an SUV travelling down the hill towards her, going as fast as the pouring rain would allow.

'Careful, mate…' She muttered the words to the unknown driver. 'Any faster and you'll be in the ditch.'

Forty feet gave her another bar on her phone, and another twenty feet one more. That should be enough. The SUV was closer now, and the driver was flashing his headlights.

'Okay, I see you.' Mimi stepped off the road, stumbling over the uneven, sticky ground.

Then she heard it. A distant rumbling sound that might have been thunder, but there had been no accompanying flash of lightning. Mimi turned in the direction of the noise, looking upstream, and then she saw its source.

'Jack…!'

She shouted into the storm, at the figure on the other side of the bridge, screaming Jack's name again when he didn't react. It was impossible to tell whether he'd heard her this time, or the thunderous sound of water rushing downstream towards him, but he turned around.

Jack took one look at the water and dropped the heavy bag he was carrying. He seemed about to try and run, but the steep slope ahead of him was slippery with mud and water.

Mimi stared in horror, unable to do anything, and knowing that Jack had only seconds to make a decision. Run for it, or find something to hang on to. There was a large spreading tree at the side of the road and she willed him towards it. As the water crashed down, she saw him run for the shelter of the tree, clinging on to one of the four split trunks which rose up from the earth.

'Jack... Hang on...' She sobbed the words even though she knew he couldn't hear them. Maybe he knew she'd be saying it, just as surely as she'd known which decision he'd make.

The noise of the water was almost deafening and, in an apocalyptic touch to the scene, the storm chose this moment to shoot a bolt of lightning through the sky, followed by a deep growl of thunder. The rush of water crashed past, taking a few chunks of the bridge with it, and Mimi kept her gaze fixed on the spot where she'd last seen Jack.

'Hang on, hang on, hang on...' It was as if she could repeat it enough times to somehow make his grip firmer. The water was subsiding now as it followed the course of the river, and she could see him, tangled in the framework of twisted tree trunks.

Maybe he was holding on or maybe unconscious; she couldn't see from here. Mimi started to run for the bridge, hoping that it hadn't been weakened too much by the impact of the water.

A voice sounded behind her but the words were whipped away in the storm. And then someone grabbed her from behind, lifting her off her feet.

'Mimi...!'

'Let go of me.' She struggled and, when he didn't let her go, she kicked against him. The feel of him was familiar, but Mimi didn't even stop to wonder how. Another sickening roar was coming from upstream.

'Jack!' She screamed his name as the second wave of water came crashing down into the valley. This one was bigger and swept the bridge away almost in one piece as the water boiled and rushed downstream.

'You can't reach him, Mimi. You'll only kill yourself.'

That voice... Maybe her mind was playing tricks on her and it wasn't him at all. But Rafe's voice was unmistakable. A trace of public school, softened by years of not caring to mark himself out as any different from the next man, and currently spiced with an urgent growl. 'Let go of me! My ambulance...'

Water spilled towards them, this time reaching the parked ambulance, pushing it sideways across the road. For a moment, Mimi thought it was going to be okay, that the vehicle would come back to rest on the tarmac, but then it slipped onto the mud by the side of the road, tipping and coming to rest against a tree, as the water retreated again.

If Jack was injured, how was she going to get him back to the hospital now? In fact, how was she going to get to him at all? The bridge was gone and the river had burst its banks and become a lethal, fast-running torrent.

'Someone's coming for him—look.' The arms

around her loosened and Mimi struggled free. She'd deal with the sick feeling in her stomach, prompted by the feel of his unrelenting body, later. She had more important things to think about right now.

She watched as five…no, six figures appeared from the trees on the other side of the river, scrambling and sliding in the mud. Two stopped to retrieve the medical bag, which had been deposited in a clump of brambles, and four made for the twisted tree trunks, where Mimi could see Jack's bright high-vis jacket.

For what seemed like an age, he lay motionless, tangled in the branches like a broken doll. One of the figures squatted down next to him as if talking to him.

Please, please, please… Yes! Through the curtain of rain, she saw him move and then Jack was helped to his feet. She strained to see as the rescue party clustered around him, and then saw him turn towards her.

'Looks as if he's still in one piece…' Rafe's voice again, behind her.

She could see that. 'Jack, are you okay? I'll meet you up at the village…' she called across.

'There's no way through, Mimi.'

'Only my friends call me Mimi.' In the sudden shock of seeing him again, all she could think about was that she wished Rafe wouldn't call her Mimi. Everyone else did, but she'd never wanted to hear him say her name ever again. If he wanted to call her something, he could call her Miriam. Or actually Ms Sawyer would be just fine.

'All right then. Miriam...' He shot her a look that told her he knew full well that she was being petty. 'We both have the same information from the control centre. Unless you're considering sprouting wings and flying...' He gestured towards the raging stream, frustration written clearly in every abrupt movement.

Mimi didn't reply. The most satisfying course of action right now was to hold Rafe responsible for both the state of the roads and the fact that her ambulance was sitting at a precarious angle in a ditch, even if that wasn't fair. Rafe had gone out of his way to teach her that life wasn't always fair.

Jack was waving and she waved back, tears springing to her eyes. Then that familiar gesture, the one she'd seen hundreds of times before. *I'll call you.* She looked around for her phone, and

Rafe picked it up from where she'd dropped it, handing it to her. Mimi took it without looking at him.

She checked that the phone was still working and then signalled back a thumbs-up to Jack. *Okay.* Then she watched him turn, as the men with him helped him back up the hill, towards the village.

Now that Jack was out of sight, she couldn't put the moment off any longer. Mimi turned to face Rafe.

He was still the same. Dark hair, wet and slicked back with one wet spike caressing his brow. Deep blue eyes, so striking that it was difficult not to stare. He still stole her breath away, and right now that felt like robbery of the cruellest kind.

If anything he seemed a little taller, but she knew that was impossible. He was staring down at her, no hint of emotion on his face, and she wondered what he saw.

'We'll wait for Jack to call, and then I'll take you back to the hospital.' Finally Rafe spoke.

'You're not taking me anywhere. My vehicle and my partner are here.'

'Your vehicle doesn't look as if it's going anywhere, and you can't get to your partner.'

Rub it in, why don't you? Rafe had clearly not forgotten how to hurt her. His strong, silent approach, unafraid to face the facts and able to make hard decisions, had been one of the things that had made Mimi notice him in the first place. But this time it wasn't up to him to make the decisions.

'It's not your call, Rafe.' If he thought that a failed relationship gave him any right to tell her what to do then he was wrong. He'd given that up five years ago, when he'd walked out on her.

'Okay. So what *are* you planning on doing?'

'I'll wait until Jack phones. Then I'll decide.' That was final, and there was nothing that Rafe could do about it.

Rafe had steeled himself against the possibility that he might bump into Mimi when he'd volunteered to help in the area. When he hadn't, he'd had to steel himself against the possibility that he might not.

Something about the way she moved had told him that it was her as he'd driven towards the figure in the rain, but he'd dismissed the idea, deciding that the woman was just another of those ghosts which had appeared before him and then turned out to be someone else. But as soon as he'd seen her start to run, he'd known. The kind of passionate loyalty that had sent her towards the wall of water instead of away from it might be foolish but it was Mimi all over and he still admired it.

Not that she'd shown very much passion when he'd left. Perhaps cool indifference was all he'd deserved after the way he'd behaved, but it had still hurt. This bristling anger, the naked hostility would have been almost refreshing if it wasn't so badly timed.

'Come and sit in the car.' He gestured back to where his SUV was parked and she glared at him. He shrugged. 'Or you could just suit yourself…'

She marched towards the car and, in a series of hurried movements, she managed to get her waterproof jacket off without getting too wet. When she was inside, she took off her overtrousers and heavy boots, hanging her coat on the clip behind her and dumping her boots in the footwell.

'I hope you don't mind my getting your car wet.'

She was sitting in the front seat frowning at him, legs drawn up in front of her, her feet in a pair of thick woolly socks. One of the things that hadn't changed about Mimi was that she was wiggling her toes. She always did that when she was unsure of her next move.

'Nope. Any time.' Rafe hung his own coat in the back of the car, and it started to drip.

'We're staying here. Until I say so, right?'

'Yes. That's right.' Mimi and Jack had always been close and always looked out for each other, but that had never inspired this sharp ache of jealousy before and it took Rafe by surprise. It had been five years. Even if it felt like just a few days since he'd last wrapped himself in her warm scent before drifting off to sleep. If she and Jack were together now, it was hardly a surprise.

She relaxed slightly into the seat. 'Might take a while. If you get tired of waiting...'

'You think I don't care about Jack?' They'd all been friends once. Whatever had happened since, Rafe still reserved the right to be concerned for him.

Her honey-brown eyes considered the question for a moment. 'No. I don't think that.'

She leaned forward, propping her phone on the dashboard, and Rafe wondered whether he should turn on the car radio to mask the silence. She looked just the same. Dark blonde hair, captured in a plait that was currently tucked into the back of her shirt. How many times had he watched her weaving it into that plait in the morning before she went to work?

'What are you doing here, Rafe?' The question had obviously been circulating in her head for a while and she didn't meet his gaze when she asked it.

'This area's the worst hit by the weather conditions. All the hospitals in the county are sparing staff where they can.'

'And you drew the short straw?'

'I volunteered.' Suddenly it seemed important that she know that. 'I'm on leave for two weeks...'

'This is your holiday?' She raised her eyebrows.

'Yeah. Beats the South of France any time.'

She gave a little nod. 'Thanks.'

The thank you was more likely to be on behalf of her hospital to his, but Rafe preferred to take it personally and think that Mimi was actually glad to see him, despite the evidence to the contrary. All the same, she seemed to be relaxing a little now.

'You and Jack are still a team, then?'

'Not for much longer. I passed my exams and I'm a qualified paramedic now.' She almost smiled. Almost but not quite.

'You're staying here to take up your promotion?'

'No, I'm moving.'

'Jack'll miss you.'

'I won't be going that far...' She broke off suddenly, staring at him. Maybe he'd been a little too obviously fishing for information. 'Who I'm going out with is none of your business, Rafe.'

'No, I know. But, out of interest, are you...and Jack?'

'Like I said, none of your business. What about you?'

'Nah. Jack's not my type.'

'I didn't mean...' The outrage drained out of her and she started to laugh. 'He'd be very glad to hear you say that.'

She fell suddenly silent, her brow creased in a frown, as if making her laugh had now become a hanging offence. Rafe settled back in his seat, watching the rain drum on the windscreen and wondering whether it was worth cracking a few more jokes, just to see how cross he could make her.

CHAPTER TWO

IT WAS A great deal easier to dislike Rafe when he wasn't around. Mimi stared gloomily at her phone, her finger tapping impatiently on the small screen.

The expected beep made her jump. A long text from an unrecognised number said that Jack was okay and in the Church Hall. He'd keep her updated as and when he knew more about the situation. And wasn't that Rafe he'd seen with her on the other side of the water?

When Mimi texted back that it was, she received a smiley face. Clearly Jack hadn't thought about the ramifications of the situation. She might have a lift home, but she would really rather have walked than it turn out to be Rafe.

She relayed the factual part of the message as dispassionately as she could, trying not to look at Rafe. The thought that she might need him wasn't particularly pleasant, but she was going to have to face facts. She'd get this over with as quickly and painlessly as possible.

Her phone beeped again. Another long text. Mimi read it carefully.

'What does he say?'

'The stuff in his medical bag's ruined. The water got to it.' Mimi had been hoping against hope that at least some of the medical equipment that Jack had been carrying would have survived the drenching. 'He's staying with the patient until he finds a way to get her out, and there are some people coming down to try and get a second bag across. We're to get it packed and ready, and wait for them to call.'

'Tell him okay.'

'Yeah.' She'd just done that. Mimi surveyed the torrent of rushing water in front of them and hoped that the people who were coming to meet them had some idea how they were going to get the bag across the river, because she didn't have a clue.

Rafe turned in his seat. 'I've got pretty much everything he might need.' He surveyed the boxes and bags in the back of the SUV. 'What's the patient's condition?'

Trust Rafe to come prepared. He always came prepared, never thinking that someone else might have the situation under control.

'She's pregnant.'

Irritation tugged at his mouth. 'I know *that.*'

'Well, that's all. She's not in labour yet, but we were going to transport her to the hospital anyway, due to the weather conditions. No complications that I know of, but best...' She was about to say that they'd best send whatever they could to deal with any eventuality, but Rafe had already got out of the car and was walking around to the tailgate. Opening it, he selected a sturdy holdall and began to stack it with boxes.

Mimi puffed out a breath and pulled her boots back on. She had no doubt that Rafe would do the right thing, or that she would, but it seemed that they were both going to do the right thing in the most unpleasant way possible.

The storm had done its worst and seemed to be easing off a little now. They didn't have to wait long before four figures appeared on the other side of the river, carrying what looked like climbing gear.

Her phone rang and she answered it.

'Hi, is that Mimi?' A woman's voice on the other end of the line, shouting over the roar of the water. 'I'm Cass… Fire and Rescue…'

At last, some good news. It was always good to have a firefighter around, even in the pouring rain.

'Hi Cass, Mimi here. How's Jack?'

'He's fine. We've taken him up to the village to dry off and we're going to try to get a line over to you now.'

'What's your plan?'

'Along the river to the east the land rises on this side. I'm thinking we may be able to throw a rope to you and winch the bag across.'

'Right you are; we'll meet you there. We have two bags.'

'That's great. Thanks.' The line cut and Mimi shouldered one of the bags. Knowing that Rafe would follow with the other, she slid carefully down the slope at the side of the road and walked into the trees.

Under the canopy of the leaves, the ground was wet but undisturbed and the clingy mud by the side of the road less in evidence. Rafe's long strides quickly caught up with her.

'There's some high ground on the other side of the river, about a quarter of a mile in this direction. They seem to think they can get a rope across.'

He nodded. Apparently he'd run out of things to say, or perhaps he'd decided that keeping the peace was the better option right now. In the silence, broken only by their footsteps and the drip of rain from the trees, Mimi resolved to do the same.

She thought she'd left this all behind. Taken charge, caught whatever life could throw at her and thrown it back. But right now she felt just as alone as she had five years ago, when Rafe had left, and still weighed down by the memories from her past.

Seventeen years old and clinging to her twin brother, Charlie, on the night they'd heard their parents had died in a car crash. Promising that they'd always be there for each other...

That promise had been kept. And, as the pain of their loss had diminished, Mimi had known that Mum and Dad would be proud of the way that she and Charlie had stuck together.

Twenty-one years old. She'd thought that she'd

been in love with Graham, and then he'd slapped her down with that list. A comprehensive catalogue of Mimi's faults and failings, which he had used to justify having slept with someone else behind her back.

She'd let him go, but somehow the list had been harder to shake. Stamped on her brain, a reminder that she was irretrievably flawed and a warning against ever trusting a man again.

But Rafe had made her believe that one last try might be possible. He had been the handsome doctor in attendance when Charlie was brought into A and E, so terribly injured, after falling from a window. It was thanks to his skill and quick action that Charlie still had some mobility left in his legs, and could pull himself up from his wheelchair and walk a few steps.

Twenty-three. When Rafe's mother had been diagnosed with cancer she'd tried so hard to support him, the way he'd supported her and Charlie, but he'd shut her out over and over again. Every day she'd felt him slip away a little more, and when he'd finally left it had been just a confirmation of everything that the list had taught her. She just wasn't good enough. And it hurt so much more to be not good enough for someone you really loved.

Mimi had picked up the pieces and set her goals. Helping Charlie regain his independence. Getting her paramedic qualification. Wiping Rafe out of her life, and never giving any man the chance to break her heart again. And she'd achieved them.

So how come she was wet through, trudging through a wood with Rafe? Feeling all the insecurities that she thought she'd put behind her. Wondering what he was thinking, and whether he might be comparing her with someone else and finding her lacking.

The straps of the bag were cutting into her shoulder and she shifted it a little. She would deal with it. She felt bad, but that had never stopped her before. It would pass. Rafe would be history again, very soon.

As they approached the place that Cass had indicated the canopy of trees thinned slightly, giving way to long grass, which had been flattened and muddied when the river broke its banks. On the other side she could see Cass's party, climbing a rocky outcrop that rose twenty feet above the level of the fast-flowing water.

'If they're going to get a line across, this is the place to do it.' Rafe had come to a halt, looking around.

'Yep.' Mimi looked up at the iron-grey sky. 'At least it's stopped raining.'

He nodded. Finally it seemed they'd found something that they could agree on.

Cass and the men on the other side were securing the end of a long rope around the trunk of a tree. She was as tall as the men with her, and seemed to be directing them. As she worked her hood fell back off her head, showing a shock of red hair, bright against the browns and dirty greens of the landscape.

Mimi's phone rang.

'We're ready.' Cass didn't bother with any preliminaries. 'I'm going to try and throw a line to you. Be ready to grab it.'

'Okay. Standing by…' Mimi looked up at Rafe. 'There's a rope coming over.'

He nodded, and Mimi saw Cass swing the rope and throw it. The coil at her feet played out, but the rope was too light to travel far and dropped into the middle of the river, immediately carried downstream by the current. The men behind her hauled it back and she tried again. It travelled further this time, dropping into the river just yards from their reach and Mimi heard Rafe puff out a breath almost at the same time as she did.

'They need to find something heavy to weight the rope...' His voice was loaded with frustration.

Mimi bit back the temptation to tell him that he was stating the obvious, and that it seemed that Cass was already doing something about it. She had to get a grip. Rafe was acting perfectly reasonably and she should at least try to be civil with him. But she was still reeling from the double shock of nearly losing Jack and then of seeing Rafe again.

She watched as Cass selected something from one of the backpacks they'd brought with them and tied it carefully on to the end of a thinner, lighter length of twine. When Cass threw again, the line came whizzing across, followed by a shout of triumph as it cleared the river, the weight dragging along the ground as the twine sank into the water and was pulled downstream.

Mimi ran for it but Rafe was faster and he was

already there, catching the weight just in time. Mimi took hold of the twine and together they dragged it clear of the water, pulling it back and winding it securely around the trunk of a tree.

Her phone rang again and there were more instructions from Cass, which Mimi relayed on to Rafe. A rope was hauled across and secured, along with clips and a pulley.

'I wonder where she got all this stuff from.' Mimi could see that the nylon ropes were strong and of high quality.

'It looks like mountaineering equipment. This is a carabiner…' Rafe was securing the rope around the tree with a no-nonsense-looking clip. 'Watch your fingers.'

'Well, give me a chance…' Mimi whipped her hand away as Rafe tested the strength of the anchor and the rope snapped tight around the tree trunk.

He waved to the party on the other bank and the bag began to move. Slowly at first, and then speeding through the air, over the water. A small pause while it was unclipped on the other side, and then the pulley came spinning back towards them.

Mimi looked at the water, boiling over jagged

rocks twenty yards downstream. She was afraid, but she wasn't going to let that stop her. She cupped her hands around her mouth, shouting across the river. 'You have a harness?'

Cass didn't seem to hear her, and Rafe shook his head.

'Leave it.' He clipped the second bag on to the pulley. As it began to move, he tugged at the ropes that anchored their end of the line around the tree trunk, assessing their strength.

Mimi knew exactly what he was thinking. Rafe was going to insist on being the one to make that perilous journey, with or without a harness. It had always been this way with him.

He'd been just the same when they'd lived together. Strong, dependable, always the first to get to grips with a problem and always the first to solve it. His quiet resourcefulness was one of the things that had drawn her to him but, after a while, standing back and watching Rafe deal with everything had begun to lose its charm.

And yet she'd done it. She couldn't bear the thought of losing Rafe and she'd tried so hard to be the woman he wanted, someone he'd think was good enough to spend his life with.

Fat lot of use that had been. His family had obviously been hoping he'd find someone from the same background as him—big house, private education, an appreciation of the finer things in life and the money to buy them. They had probably heaved a joint sigh of relief when Rafe had left her.

She wasn't about to let Rafe walk all over her again. 'I'll go first. I'm lighter than you are.' She spoke casually, even though she knew that the words would be like a red rag to a bull.

'You will not.'

'Just watch me, Rafe.' She threw the retort at him, watching as the group across the river retrieved the second bag. As they did so, a crack sounded across the water. One of the ropes came whipping towards them and she felt herself falling sideways as Rafe tackled her to the ground. The rope described an arc in the air above their heads and flopped down next to them.

'Ow! Did you have to do that?' Mimi rolled away from him, straight into a patch of mud. She'd been trying so hard to show him that he didn't need to protect her any more. Rafe sweeping her off her feet, however dispassionately he'd done it, was the last thing she needed.

'Nope. Could have just let it take your head off.' He had the audacity to grin at her.

'I'm beginning to wish you had.' She brushed herself down, resisting the temptation to thank him. Instead she turned to the group on the other side of the river, who were standing motionless, staring across at them.

Mimi took her phone out of her pocket, dialling Cass's number.

'Sorry about that. You okay?' Cass's voice sounded down the line.

'Yes, fine.' Rafe was behind her, muttering something about tying her to a tree to keep her out of trouble, and she ignored him. 'I'm going to try to get to you. I might be able to get through on the other road into the village...'

'I doubt anyone's going to get through safely tonight.' There was a pause. 'Jack said that he's getting in contact with the HEMS team. When the rain gives over a bit they might be able to make it. If there's anything he needs, you'll be the first to know.'

That was sensible. And, coming from Cass,

it didn't sound like a put-down. 'Okay, thanks. Give him my love...'

'Will do. When this is over, there's a bottle of red with our name on it, if you fancy a night out.'

'I'll be there.' She waved across to the group on the other side of the river and ended the call. Thankfully, Rafe had decided not to make good on his threats and was already unclipping the remaining rope from around the tree, watching as it was hauled back across the water.

'We're going.' It was an obvious statement, but it made Mimi feel good to be the one to say it. Turning away from him, she started to walk back towards the road as the rain started falling again.

They made the journey in silence. Perhaps Rafe was figuring out what he was going to save her from next. When they reached the stricken ambulance, he walked over to it.

'I don't think I'm going to be able to tow you out...' He was peering underneath the vehicle. 'In any case, it looks as if there's a fair bit of damage, here.'

'I'm going to call for a tow truck.' *Thanks, Rafe, but you're no longer needed. You can go now.* Treacherous regret tugged at Mimi's heart at the thought.

'Don't forget the CD safe.' There was a barb in his tone.

No, she hadn't forgotten the controlled drugs that the ambulance carried, and she did know that she had to remove them.

'I'll let you get on.' She turned, making for the back doors of the ambulance, and felt his grip on her arm.

'Let me go, Rafe.' She pulled against him, but he didn't relent.

'What are you expecting me to do? Leave you here with no shelter and no transport?' He gave an incredulous shake of his head. 'Think again.'

'Let. Go.' Every time he touched her, it was the same. The memories were almost like solid, living things, tearing at her heart and reminding her that once upon a time, in a land far, far away, she'd craved Rafe's touch.

He uncurled his fingers from her wrist. Not too fast, not too slow. Rafe had always been a master of the art of good timing.

'Stay if you must. I'm calling for the tow truck.' She forced herself to look away from him, scrolling through the list of numbers on her phone for the vehicle recovery company.

If he had to put a name to that look, Rafe supposed that hostile arousal might just about cover it. He had no doubt that the hostility was there, but the arousal was probably just wishful thinking on his part.

He supposed he didn't deserve anything else, but she didn't have to ram it down his throat. It was obvious that she could cope without him, but he wasn't entirely surplus to requirements. If she thought that leaving her hadn't hurt him as well, then she could think again.

Rafe kicked disgruntledly at the tyre of the disabled ambulance. Mimi had taken hold of her life with both hands, gained a qualification and got a new job. His life was back on track, too. When he'd left, he'd made the right decision and now was no time to start re-examining it.

The ambulance was tipped at a slight angle in the mud, but it was wedged firmly against a tree and seemed stable enough. Rafe gave the vehicle a good shove and it stayed put, so gingerly he opened the back doors and climbed inside, looking around to assess the damage.

'They're sending a truck out. The tow company's pretty busy, but they're giving me priority, so they should be here inside an hour.' She was standing in the rain, outside the ambulance, looking at him thoughtfully.

'Good. Not long to wait, then.' This couldn't be easy for her. Medicine was all about teamwork, and he knew that the nature of the ambulance crews' work tended to forge the tightest of teams. She must be feeling very alone right now.

She looked up at him and he thought he saw a flicker of confused warmth in her face. 'How much of the ambulance equipment can you take in your car?'

'Pretty much everything that's portable.' Rafe surveyed the inside of the wrecked vehicle. 'Apart from the stretcher.'

'I was reckoning on leaving that.' Mimi was standing stock-still, her arms folded. As if she knew what she had to do but just couldn't bring herself to start. Rafe picked up one of the bags, stowed away under the seat, and climbed out of the stricken vehicle, making his way to his car.

* * *

Rafe's sudden appearance seemed to have peeled away everything she had built up in the last five years, like a bad skin graft sloughing off a wound, leaving it red raw. And now she was leaving Jack behind and stripping her ambulance of everything that could be moved. She could almost reach out and touch the feeling of loss.

She *had* to get a grip. Mimi repeated the words in her head, in the hope that they might sink in.

As usual, it was practically impossible to see what Rafe was thinking, but as they worked quietly together the atmosphere between them seemed to relax. He watched as she checked through the contents of the Controlled Drugs safe, countersigning the inventory, and then set to work helping stow as much as they could from the ambulance into his car.

Typically, the rain seemed to slacken off just as they were finishing, and the tow truck chose that moment to arrive as well. Tired and shivering, Mimi clambered into Rafe's car and hung her dripping jacket in the back.

'Here.' He rummaged for a moment on the back

seat, unzipped a bag and produced a sweater. 'Put this on.'

He ducked back out of the car, closing the door, and Mimi picked up the sweater. She didn't particularly want to follow his orders, nor did she want to wear his clothes, but refusing might give him the idea it meant something to her. And when she pulled it over her head it was warm and all-enveloping.

The key was in the ignition and she started the engine, putting the heaters on full and directing the ventilation up on to the windows. As they began to clear she could see Rafe, talking to the vehicle recovery men as the winch slowly pulled her ambulance out of the mud and on to the back of the truck.

He jogged back to the car and got in. 'I'm ready whenever you are.'

'Yes. Let's go.' She blurted out the instruction, knowing that he wouldn't go anywhere unless she allowed it, and realising that somehow that didn't put her in charge.

'Hospital?'

'Yes, thanks. We need to get the controlled drugs back there.'

He nodded, leaning forward to start the engine. Even in these conditions it wouldn't take long before they were back at the hospital and then she could thank him and wave him goodbye.

CHAPTER THREE

RAFE WAITED WHILE Mimi argued with the ambulance control supervisor. They'd both turned around at the same time, to look at him for a moment, and then Mimi had turned away again, her eyes dead, as if he mattered rather less to her than the chair he was sitting on. The supervisor beckoned her into his office and she followed him, protest leaking from every movement she made.

He'd loved her fire. That unquenchable, unstoppable thirst for life that made the best out of everything had enchanted Rafe. It had challenged all the assumptions that his family had taught him. *Boys don't cry. A man should take care of the women in his life. He must handle his problems alone, not needing to talk about them.*

And Rafe had come so close to quenching that fire. When his mother had been diagnosed with cancer, and his family had descended into a state of restrained crisis, Mimi had wanted to help, had fought him to let her in. But Rafe couldn't. He'd already perfected the art of hiding whatever pain life threw at him and he didn't know how to do anything else.

He didn't blame her for giving up on him, but it had hurt all the more because Mimi never gave up on anything. Lying with her in their bed, unable to either sleep or to share his anguish, had taught Rafe the nature of true loneliness. Leaving had been his way of keeping her safe from the silence that had descended on their home.

That was all history now. He'd thought it could never change but, as the door of the supervisor's office opened and he saw Mimi walk towards him, he began to wonder. He'd measured his failure in their relationship by the lack of emotion she'd shown when he left, but now anger was stamped all over her face and he had little doubt that most of it was directed at him.

'Everything okay?'

She shook her head. 'There are no spare vehicles and no one for me to partner with. They're sending me home...'

'Unless?' Rafe had seen enough of the situation here to be able to guess what Mimi's options were.

Her face was set in an expression of almost believable remorse. 'I apologise for what I said. I should have thanked you for getting me out of the way of that rope when it broke.'

Mimi was still thinking about *that*? Then Rafe realised that this was the precursor to something else.

'You're welcome. I apologise for what I said too. I had no real intention of tying you to a tree.' However appealing the thought had been at the time.

'No. It didn't really occur to me that you did. I think we were both letting off a bit of steam.' She screwed her face into a frown. 'My controller... He says that if you need any help I could always tag along with you.'

Deep down inside a primitive sense of triumph pulled at him. However much she disliked the idea, Mimi needed him. Rafe tried to think dispassionately. Two would be more effective than one, and he'd be able take more calls. Unless, of course, they spent the rest of the evening bickering over old grudges.

'Do you think that's going to work?'

Mimi took a deep breath, as if she was suppressing the urge to solve the problem by killing him and taking his car keys. 'I'll make it work, Rafe. I can't sit this out; I'll go crazy at home.'

There wasn't even a decision to make. Turning down any assistance, let alone that of a trained paramedic, would be reckless at a time like this. 'Happy to have you along. I'd appreciate the help.'

That was that, then. There was a lot of unresolved anger between them, but if they could put that aside this could work.

They stood for a moment staring at each other and then Mimi broke the silence.

'Look, this is difficult, but we could make it a lot easier.'

'Yeah, I guess we could. I'd like that...' Rafe remembered not to call her *Mimi* this time. That was just the kind of thing that might shatter this unstable truce.

'We'll make a new start, shall we?'

Pretend that none of it had ever happened? That he hadn't loved her and then left her, and that resentment wasn't colouring everything they did now. It was a tough prospect, but if that was what it took... It was, in fact, an opportunity. If there *was* unfinished business between them, then maybe now was the time to finish it for good.

'Yes. Okay, I'd like that. New start.'

Mimi felt better now that she'd had a chance to wash her face and comb her hair. She folded Rafe's sweater, making a conscious effort not to bury her face into its softness, trying to catch one last trace of his scent. This was hard.

She stuffed the sweater into a bag, dragged her jacket on and marched out into the rain. He was sitting in the car, waiting for her. Her colleague. The one she'd slept with once upon a time, but that had been a mistake and it was all finished now.

'Ready?' She settled herself into the front seat of the car.

He nodded, turning the radio down until it was just a gentle beat, swallowed up by the drumming of the rain on the windscreen. 'Yep. First one's near Shillingford. We'll have to go through Eardwell.'

Her home village. 'Yes, that's the best way.'

'You want to call in on Charlie?'

'He's...I spoke to him a few minutes ago. He says everything's okay.' Mimi wished that Charlie would accept her help a little more readily, but she knew better than to fuss.

'How's he doing?'

'A lot better. He plays in a wheelchair basketball team now.'

'Sounds as if he's a great deal more independent.'

'Yeah. As time went by we all learned how to make that happen.' The cottage that she and Rafe had rented, just across the road from Charlie's place, had been a factor in that. Close enough to help, without crowding her brother. When Rafe had said he was moving, to take up a new job and be closer to his mother, he'd known full well that Mimi couldn't abandon Charlie and follow him.

'I don't suppose he's got a spare flask he can lend us. If he could fill it up with coffee it would be even better.'

She couldn't help but smile. Rafe and Charlie had always got on well, and it seemed that Rafe still cared about her brother enough to find an excuse to pop in and see whether he was all right. 'You want a sandwich as well?'

'Sounds good. Call him and tell him we're coming.' Rafe swung the car out of the hospital car park and on to the road.

Rafe drove the familiar route, which he'd used to call the road home. He hadn't reckoned on it being quite so hard. When he stopped outside their cottage, it looked just the same as it always had, the white render gleaming pale in the pouring rain like a ghost from his past.

'You're still here?' He tried to make the question sound as casual as possible, as if there hadn't been a time when he had dreamed about walking back to that door every night.

There was a slight pause, as if she was weighing up whether it was all right to answer. 'Yes. I bought the place.'

'Mrs Bates died?' The elderly woman who had owned the cottage had gone into a nursing home and her family had rented the property out.

'Yes. Four years ago. The family didn't want the cottage and decided to sell, so I put in an offer.'

'Smart move...' Rafe bit his tongue. He wasn't in a position to give Mimi advice on what to do with her life any more. All the same, he'd thought more than once that if the roomy cottage they'd rented ever came on to the market they should put in an offer for it.

She nodded as if she didn't want to discuss it any more, and rather unnecessarily pointed to the driveway of Charlie's one-storey house, right across the road. It had only been five years, not a century. And Rafe hadn't forgotten.

He got as close to the front door as he could and switched the engine off, leaning back in his seat in an unequivocal signal that he'd wait. Turning up here with Mimi wasn't the most tactful of things to do.

'Come and say hello to Charlie.' She shot him a pretty fair counterfeit of a welcoming smile.

'I thought… Wouldn't you prefer me to stay here?'

'I told him you were here when I spoke to him. He's not going to eat you, Rafe.'

Maybe he would and maybe he wouldn't. But Rafe had often wondered how Charlie was doing and he wanted to see him. Mimi had already got out of the car and was running up the ramp which led to the front door, her jacket over her head. It opened as she approached and Rafe saw Charlie inside.

Rafe swung out of his seat, following Mimi to the front door. Charlie looked great. Strong and smiling as he pulled Mimi down for a kiss. 'You just couldn't resist, could you...'

'What?' Mimi broke free, giving a look which was far too innocent to be believed, and Charlie grinned at her.

'Couldn't resist checking up on me.'

'All I want is coffee. Then we'll go. If you want you can go lie on the floor and I'll step over you on the way out.' Mimi turned her back on her brother and walked towards the kitchen area at the far end of the open-plan space.

'You can finish making the sandwiches...' Charlie called after her and then turned his attention to Rafe, his face suddenly impassive. 'You're back then.'

'I'm here to help out, that's all.' Mimi seemed to be busy in the kitchen and Charlie was showing no inclination towards following her. Rafe sat down. If Charlie wanted to give him the third degree, he could do it face to face.

'I hear that Jack's marooned, and the ambulance was towed?' Charlie seemed to be fishing for information, and Rafe guessed that Mimi hadn't told him the whole story.

'Yeah, that's right. The river broke its banks near Holme and the bridge has been washed away. Jack got pretty wet, but we hear he's okay. Mimi had walked back up the hill to make a phone call.'

'Yeah. That's what I heard too. Did she try to get across the river?'

'She… Perhaps you should ask her.'

Charlie leaned forward. 'I'm asking *you*, Rafe.'

'I thought she might. I didn't give her the choice.' Rafe decided that telling Charlie he'd had to lift Mimi off her feet before she ran headlong towards a wall of water wasn't a particularly good idea. And if she hadn't mentioned anything about her plans for getting across the river he'd keep quiet about them as well.

'Yeah. I reckoned that's what happened.' Charlie seemed to relax a bit. 'Thanks.'

'My pleasure. Although I'm not sure it was Mi…Miriam's.' Mimi's full name sounded strange and very cold on his lips, but Rafe had made up his mind to play it safe and use it, since she seemed to object so much to his using her nickname.

'Miriam…?' Charlie's face broke into a grin. 'She *is* giving you a hard time, isn't she?'

'Do you blame her?' Somehow Rafe couldn't quite leave it at that. 'There were reasons, Charlie. For my leaving…'

'I dare say there were. That's between you and Mimi. She told me to mind my own business enough times.'

A quiver of unexpected warmth jabbed at Rafe's heart. Mimi could have said whatever she liked about him, and it was only to be expected that she'd bad-mouthed him to Charlie. He hadn't realised until this moment how much he'd wanted her not to.

'Do me a favour, though…' Charlie interrupted his reverie.

'Of course.' Rafe had absolutely no intention of trying to rekindle anything between him and Mimi, and sex for old times' sake definitely wasn't on his agenda. He could reassure Charlie on that score, at least.

'I know Mimi's job has risks attached to it, and

I also know she doesn't tell me about half the scrapes she gets herself into...'

'They're not scrapes, Charlie, and she doesn't get herself into them. She's a trained professional.' Rafe surprised himself by springing to Mimi's defence.

'Yeah, I know.' Charlie ran his hand through his hair. 'Look after her, will you? You know Mimi. She thinks she's superwoman sometimes.'

'You have my word on that.' Rafe held out his hand, wondering if Charlie would take it. He did so without hesitation. He was so like Mimi, in both looks and mannerism, and it felt doubly warming that Charlie seemed ready to forgive.

'It's good to see you.' Charlie's irrepressible grin broke through his reserve. 'I've missed our little talks.'

Rafe chuckled. Their *little talks* usually lasted until closing time in the local pub, when Mimi was working a late shift. 'Me too. We should do it again some time.'

'Yeah. That would be good.'

Things were going okay. Not good, but okay. They were adults and there was no reason in the world why she and Rafe couldn't play nicely until the situation eased. There was just one thing that needed clearing up.

'I heard what you said to Charlie.'

'Yeah?' He didn't turn his gaze from the road ahead but Mimi supposed she shouldn't expect that. She wouldn't have done if she'd been driving either.

'It's quite unnecessary.'

'Which bit of it in particular?'

'About looking after me. There's no need.'

Rafe's shoulders moved in a tight shrug. 'You want me to go back on my word?'

'Far be it from me to get in the way of any male bonding that you've been engaging in, but I'd rather you didn't involve me in it.' Mimi shut her mouth tight. That sounded sharper than it should, but when she'd heard Rafe and Charlie's quiet words she'd felt a little more hurt than she should too.

'I didn't say it to impress Charlie. It's what I intend to do.' The side of his jaw hardened in an obstinate line. She knew that look, and it had frustrated her when she'd been living with him. She didn't need to put up with it any more.

'I've been looking after myself for the last five years, Rafe, and I've met all the challenges that life can throw at me. I'm sorry if that tears a hole in your masculinity, but that's the way things are. I don't need you to look after me, and I'd appreciate it if you didn't go around pretending that I did.'

She felt a little breathless. Almost free, as if that was something that she'd been waiting for a long time to say. Mimi dismissed the idea. There was nothing…nothing that she'd been waiting to say to Rafe.

The car suddenly pulled off the road, jerking to a halt. 'You think this is all about my ego?'

'Well, it's not about mine…' The atmosphere was zinging with hurt antagonism.

'Not about you?' He turned around to face her and she saw her own anger reflected in his face. 'We all need each other at the moment. If you can't deal with that then that's all about you.'

'Stop trying to twist things around, Rafe…'

'I am *not* twisting anything. And I didn't promise Charlie that I'd look after you because you're a woman, *or* because we used to sleep together.'

Mimi caught her breath. He'd said the words

they'd both been trying not to say. The words that could lead to all kinds of trouble…*we used to sleep together.* After all the efforts she'd been making not to think about it.

'That's all ancient history.'

His lip curled in disbelief, and suddenly he was very close. That scent of his, a little soap, a little sweat. She'd always loved the way that Rafe smelled, and it was just as intoxicating as it had always been.

'We need to get one thing straight. It's fine with me if you just want to come along for the ride. I happen to think that would be a shame, because I was hoping that I could rely on you.'

'What for?' The words almost stuck in her throat. Suddenly she couldn't think of one thing that Rafe would want to rely on her for.

'You know these roads better than I do. You know the best way to get to where we need to go. And you have a lot of experience of working with people outside the hospital, which I don't have. I could really do with your help.'

'I…I want to help.' Although they'd worked at the same hospital for over a year, Mimi had never worked with Rafe. She knew he was a fine doctor and had often wished she could have that opportunity.

'Right then. So we're a team?'

'Yes... That would be good.'

'In that case, I get to look out for you. The same way that I hope you'll look out for me.'

Mimi swallowed hard. 'You want *me* to look out for *you*?'

'Why not?' His sudden grin burned into her soul like a red-hot brand. 'It's expensive to train new doctors. You'd be doing the economy a favour.'

Right now, the economy was the last thing on her mind. She tried to drag her attention away from the curve of his lips.

'Okay then—partners. I'll look after you and you can look after me.'

He held out his hand and she took it, almost in a dream. One of those bright, happy dreams that had so often been shattered when she woke and found that Rafe wasn't sleeping next to her.

'Partners it is, then.'

Suddenly the dream cracked. Mimi had promised herself not to risk falling for another man and fantasising about Rafe, of all people, was plain crazy.

She let go of his hand, settling back into her seat. Five years ago she'd been foolish enough to believe that she meant something to him, and now... He'd be gone soon and he wouldn't look back.

Perhaps that was the advantage of having a heart that had once been broken. It was stronger now, and well defended. Rafe couldn't just walk back into her life and steal it.

The shining look on her face, the way her lips were parted slightly, had obliterated everything else. Mimi might be as tough as they came, but when she made love she was the softest, sweetest thing.

Don't do this. Don't even think about it.

He'd made one promise to Charlie, and another to himself. He wasn't going to break either of them. Rafe switched on the engine, jamming the car into first gear with more force than was strictly necessary, and started to drive.

CHAPTER FOUR

THEIR FIRST CALL was to a man with cuts and bruises, from where a dry-stone wall had collapsed onto him. In better circumstances he might well have just turned up in A and E, but he'd called first and been passed on to the Disaster Control Team, who had told him to stay put and wait for someone to get to him.

With Rafe there, it was possible to treat him in situ. Not the best use of his skills, but it saved time and resources where they were needed the most. The kitchen table was turned into a temporary treatment area, and Eric's arm lay supported on a wad of dressing as Rafe carefully injected the local anaesthetic on either side of the wound.

'You're the doctor's assistant?' Eric's wife came to sit next to Mimi at the other end of the long table.

'No.' She flipped her gaze towards Rafe to check that he wasn't grinning and saw that his concentration was wholly on what he was doing. 'I'm a paramedic. Only my ambulance got washed away in the river.'

'Up by Holme? I heard about that on the local radio news; they're completely cut off now. No one hurt, I hope.'

'No. Just got a bit wet.'

A baby started to cry in the other room and the woman hurried out, returning with her child in her arms. 'We're sorry to bring you out all this way. Eric was going to go into A and E, but I was worried about him driving and I called first. They said they'd send a doctor to us.' Her tone was apologetic.

'That's all right. We're trying to get as many people as possible treated at home because A and E is pretty stretched at the moment. It's a lot better this way, all round.'

'Not for you. It looks as if it's going to be a filthy night again.' The woman turned the edges of her mouth down in sympathy, and Mimi smiled.

'I'll be in bed, drinking cocoa and reading a book soon enough.' Mimi thought she saw a movement from Rafe out of the corner of her

eye, but when she turned he was already looking away again.

'Whatever you earn you deserve more...' Eric
broke in, and his wife nodded.

'I tell my boss that all the time.' Mimi grinned,
picking up a soft toy from the table and waggling
it in front of the baby. There wasn't much else
for her to do. 'What do you say to my making a
cup of tea?'

'Tea?' Rafe seemed to hear the magic word.
'That would be nice, thanks.'

Mimi swallowed the temptation to tell him that
the tea was intended for their patient. Picking the
kettle up and finding it empty, she went to fill it
up at the sink.

Rafe stood at the end of the path, surveying the
small cottage for any signs of life, and Mimi
knocked on the door again. No answer.

'I don't suppose we've got the wrong address...?'

'Nope. This is the right one.' Mimi bent down
to shout through the letterbox. 'Toby. Open the
door.'

Obviously she'd been here before. Or maybe

she knew the elderly man who lived here. They'd been summoned by a concerned neighbour, who had noticed that he was limping and had seen an infected sore on his leg.

'Do you think he might not be able to get to the door?' Rafe suggested, wondering if they were going to have to break in.

'Shouldn't think so. He's probably hiding out in the kitchen.' Mimi walked to the side of the cottage, squeezing through the narrow space between the wall and a waterlogged hedge, and Rafe followed, avoiding the branches that sprung back behind her.

She clambered over a low wall, walking past a small kitchen garden to the back door. He stopped and waited, reckoning that Mimi probably knew what she was doing. She pressed her face against the glass, rattling the handle.

'Toby, open up.'

There was a short pause, and Mimi banged on the door again. Then it opened, to reveal an elderly man.

'You might have said it was you…'

'Can we come in, Toby?'

'You'd better. You'll catch your death out there.'

Mimi entered and Rafe hung back from the door as Toby eyed him suspiciously.

'This is Dr Chapman.'

'Where's the other lad?'

'Jack's up at the top of the hill, in Holme. He's a bit tied up at the moment.'

Toby nodded sagely and beckoned Rafe inside. A black and white collie was sleeping by the fire and raised its head to inspect the visitors, then rested it back onto its front paws. The little kitchen was old-fashioned, yet clean and neat as a new pin.

'What can I do for you?' Toby sat down at the kitchen table, its polished surface dark and pitted from years of use.

'Mrs March called us. She says you've got something wrong with your leg.' Mimi's tone was firm, but she was smiling.

'It's nothing.' The old man's chin jutted in a show of defiance. His face was like the surface of the table, dark from years spent in the open air, with deep lines at the side of his eyes.

'No, probably not. But the thing is, now I'm here I have to have a look at it. Those are the rules.'

'And him?' Toby gestured in Rafe's direction.

Mimi looked around, a trace of the smile that she'd bestowed on Toby still lingering on her face. After the uneasy truce between them, which seemed to have started to crumble as soon as it was made, it was like a ray of sunshine. 'Yeah, he's got to look at it as well.'

Toby sniffed. 'One of you not good enough, then.'

Mimi directed a bright grin at Toby and the old man's face softened. 'Come on, Toby. Give me a break, eh?'

Toby shrugged and Mimi knelt down in front of him, pulling a pair of gloves from her pocket and carefully rolling Toby's trouser leg up. Halfway up his calf, a large sore blazed red against the pallor of his skin.

'Have you been wading in flood water?' Mimi voiced the first question which occurred to Rafe. Flood water frequently carried a high concentration of bacteria, and in the circumstances it was the most likely candidate for turning a small injury into an angry, obviously infected wound like this.

'Mebbe...' Toby shrugged non-committally.

'I'll take that as a yes. You've been with your grandson up at the farm, have you?'

'The lad needed some help to get all the animals inside. The pasture's waterlogged.'

'And when was this?'

'Day before yesterday.'

'Okay. This looks as if it hurts.' Mimi gave Toby no chance to reply, clearly suspecting that he wasn't about to admit it if it did. 'I'd like the doctor to take a look at it, and he'll tell us what needs to be done.'

Toby raised one eyebrow, pursed his lips and regarded Rafe steadily. The effect was something like the assessing stare of his first tutor, back when he was a student. Rafe took his coat off, hanging it on the back of one of the kitchen chairs, and bent to examine the leg.

'Yes, there's some infection there.' Rafe stated the obvious and tried not to notice that Mimi was rolling her eyes. 'I'll get some antibiotics and we'll dress the wound...'

'That's okay. I'll get them.' Mimi was on her feet already. 'I'll pop in to see Mrs March on the way, and I need to make a phone call.'

'Okay, thanks.' Rafe supposed that the visit

next door and the phone call were going to be about making sure that Toby was looked in on every day. The wound would heal, but not if he didn't take care of it. She caught up her coat and breezed through to the front door, leaving Rafe and Toby staring at each other.

'Nice girl. Reminds me of my Joan.' Toby broke the silence.

'This is her?' Rafe craned over to look at the photograph on the sideboard, and Toby nodded. 'She's beautiful.'

'That she was. Right up until the day she died.' Toby's eyes lingered for a moment on the image. 'Had a temper, like your girl.'

'She's not my girl. We're just working together.'

Toby gave a short barked laugh. 'My Joan and me, we used to argue like cat and dog, but we never let the sun go down on a quarrel. Five kids to show for it, and twelve grandkids.'

'Sounds like good advice.' Rafe wondered what Toby would think of letting things simmer for five years.

'It is. You and your girl...'

'She's not my girl, Toby.'

'Aye. Well, take your eyes off her when she's

not looking, and look her in the face when she is, and then I might believe you.'

There was no answer to that. Not one that Rafe could think of anyway, and that allowed Toby to warm to his theme.

'Sun's almost down. Puts you on borrowed time.'

Rafe had been congratulating himself that, whatever their private differences, neither he nor Mimi had allowed them to bleed into their work and they'd remained entirely professional in front of their patients. But it appeared that he'd been mistaken.

'It's…complicated.' Rafe decided that denials weren't going to work this time. Toby might be elderly, but that was no reason to treat him as if he was stupid.

'No, it's not. You find a girl you like and, if she likes you, you lead her up the hill to the church.' Toby folded his arms in a gesture of finality.

The front door slammed, saving Rafe from the difficult task of working out how to answer that. Mimi's footsteps sounded in the hall and Toby twisted around in his seat as she appeared in the kitchen doorway.

'Right. I've spoken to Mrs March and she's given me your daughter's number.' She waved a piece of paper at Toby and put the dressings down on the table, avoiding Rafe's gaze when he went to thank her. He wondered if she watched him when he wasn't looking, and wished he'd thought to ask Toby.

'Are you going to call her, or would you like me to do it?' Mimi gave Toby her most persuasive smile.

'Since you've come all this way, best you do something.' Toby's retort was accompanied by a slight gleam in his eye.

'Yeah, right. Because you wouldn't want me to be bored while the doctor sees to your leg.' Mimi grinned at him good-humouredly and pulled out her phone, turning her back on Rafe as she dialled the number.

He had been about to ask Mimi to assist him, but apparently he was going to have to juggle scissors, tape and a dressing pad on his own. That wasn't what worried Rafe. What worried him was the feeling that he and Mimi weren't so much working together as working in close proximity to each other.

He disinfected the wound and dressed it, then broke open the blister pack, taking the first of the antibiotic tablets out. 'Take this one now. Then three times a day for the next week. It should start to feel better in a couple of days, but if it gets any worse call us again.'

'Wasn't me as called you the first time.' Now that Toby was reassured about his leg, a mischievous sense of humour had begun to surface. Mimi remonstrated with him and, after another short battle of wills, it was time to pack up and go.

'You know him?' Rafe asked as he settled back behind the wheel of the car.

'Yeah. He broke his hip about three years ago, up at his grandson's farm, and Jack and I attended. I went to see how he was doing in hospital, and he had all the nurses wound around his little finger. When he got better, he turned up at the ambulance station with two bags of home-grown strawberries, one each for me and Jack.'

'Nice.'

'They were. They had a real flavour to them, not like the ones you get in the supermarket.' Even though they were alone in the car, Mimi's smile wasn't for him. It was for Toby and the strawberries, and maybe for Jack. She must be missing Jack.

Rafe reminded himself that he shouldn't need her smile in order to work effectively. Despite all their good intentions, he and Mimi just weren't functioning as a team and they needed to address that. Quickly, if Toby was to be believed, because the sun was going down. He leaned back in his seat, trying to think of some way to broach the subject casually.

'So, marks out of ten. What would you give us?' Rafe accompanied the words with a smile, hoping that it would soften them. 'I reckon ten out of ten for individual performances, and a lot less for teamwork.'

She coloured suddenly. 'What do you mean?'

'Well, how many marks out of ten do you give *me* for teamwork?'

Mimi shrugged. 'Can't we leave the psych assessments until later?'

Something in her tone made Rafe press the point. 'I'd say one. Two if I was being generous. How many marks do you give yourself?'

She turned her gaze on him, luminous in the

gathering dusk. Her eyes, wide and dark, seemed almost to be pleading with him.

'I…I probably don't deserve any more than one. But I can do better.' Her words were almost a whisper.

She looked so deflated, so hurt, that he instinctively reached out for her, stopping only a moment away from touching her hand. The problem was almost entirely of his making and he'd blundered in, trying to fix it. And somehow all he'd managed to do was to wound Mimi.

'It's me that needs to do better, not you.' Mimi looked as if she was on the edge of tears and the impulse to comfort her was almost irresistible.

None of his old coping strategies were going to work. Rafe knew that he needed to try something new.

'We need to talk.'

She was doing it again, judging herself, doing herself down, before Rafe got the chance. And now he wanted to talk? Somewhere in the universe, something very big must have jolted out of alignment because Rafe didn't talk.

Even though she'd cursed him a million times

in her head for not sharing how he felt, now that he'd offered she didn't want to hear it. The thought that Rafe's list might be far more damning than anything which Graham might have concocted terrified her.

'You want *me*...?' She couldn't even say it.

'I'll give it a go if you will.' His voice was suddenly tender. 'We're both so busy doing our own thing that... Well, neither of us has put a foot wrong with a patient yet, but that might be only a matter of time. I want to do better, and I'd like you to help me.'

There wasn't enough air in here. Her heart was labouring and her head was spinning.

But he was right. They had too much baggage, and it could so easily blind them to something important.

'We...can't do it now.' She needed some time to think.

'No. Later?'

She looked at her watch. 'It's eight o'clock...' It would take them at least another two hours to get through the calls they already had. She would rather have the option of going with him to a pub or a coffee bar, but they'd barely make it before closing time. 'Are you staying in town tonight?'

'I've got one of the on-call rooms at the hospital.'

That wasn't going to work either. The last thing that Mimi wanted was to be overheard by anyone there. She needed to be clear about what she was offering, though. 'Before you go back there, you can come to my place. Just…half an hour.'

'Thanks. I'd really appreciate that.'

CHAPTER FIVE

THE MOOD HAD lightened between them. It was eleven o'clock before they had worked through the list of calls they had to make, but they'd done it. There had even been a couple of bad jokes, which they'd both laughed far too loudly over in an attempt to prove that they were at ease with the situation. Rafe knew that, in reality, about the only thing that they shared any more was the certain knowledge that what lay ahead of them wasn't going to be easy.

He was about to swing into the parking space to one side of the cottage, and then realised that this was no longer his home.

'Where can I park?'

'Use the hardstanding. My car's at the hospital.'

He should have thought of that and offered to take her there, so she could drive it back here, but it was too late now. He manoeuvred the heavy vehicle into the tight space and switched off the engine.

'Is this okay? If you're tired...'

'It's okay.' She seemed to have screwed her courage up for this, and he knew Mimi didn't back down. She got out of the car, and made a dash for the porch, unlocking the front door and not looking behind her as she disappeared inside. Rafe followed her, trying not to drip too much water on to the hall floor.

When they'd rented this place together, the decor had been gloomy and tired and Rafe had asked if he could apply a few licks of paint. The landlord had agreed willingly, and he and Mimi had chosen a cream colour for the walls, with an oatmeal-coloured carpet to match. She'd hung a few pictures and suddenly the place had become clean and welcoming.

Now, it was like a different place altogether. She'd ripped up the carpet and laid a wooden floor instead, and the walls were painted a faded plum colour, which suited the age of the cottage perfectly. An old dresser, which looked as if it had been lovingly restored and polished, stood in place of the flat-pack hall table.

She took off her coat and motioned for him to come through. Rafe followed her into the kitchen. Here, the new cabinets he'd put in were gone too, the wooden doors replaced with shiny white ones. No better, no worse. Just completely different.

'Hang your coat here. It'll dry off a bit.' She pulled a chair that he didn't recognise away from a table he didn't recognise, and put it close to the old wood-burning stove, which was about the only thing that still remained from when he'd lived here. Rafe imagined that it had gained a reprieve only by dint of being too large and too heavy for Mimi to disconnect and drag out of the house.

He sat down, watching as she took cups from the cupboard and boiled the kettle. Rafe had taken nothing with him when he'd moved out, just his clothes and personal belongings, reckoning that the least he owed Mimi was to leave the home that they'd built together behind for her. She hadn't wanted it, though. Even the cups and the tea towels were different.

'You've made a good job of the place.' His first instinct was still to hide his feelings and pretend that nothing had happened, but he was trying to do things differently. If he couldn't quite bring himself to tell her how much it hurt to see how ruthlessly she'd expunged any sign that he'd ever been here, he could at least acknowledge that there was a change.

'Thanks.' She looked around the kitchen thoughtfully, seeming to decide that saying nothing was her best option.

'So you've been studying, renovating the cottage and looking out for Charlie.' Rafe imagined that every penny she earned and every moment of her time must have gone into those three things. 'Anything else? You must have had at least five minutes' spare time since I saw you last.'

Her face broke into a sudden smile. 'It was six minutes. And I wasted them quite shamelessly, eating chocolate in front of the TV.'

A faint echo of the life they'd had together here smacked Rafe squarely on the jaw. The evenings when she'd raided her not-so-secret chocolate stash and curled up on the sofa with him, feeding him the odd square as they talked. 'I'm glad to hear it.'

She threw the tea bags into the cups and made

the tea, giving each one a perfunctory stir before carrying them over to the table. She seemed to be about to sit down and then had second thoughts, clearly unwilling to go to the lengths of sharing a table with him just yet.

He should give a bit more. Something about his own life, perhaps. 'I'm working at the new emergency care unit at Hartsholme Hospital.'

Surprise registered on her face. 'I heard about that. I gather there's some groundbreaking work going on there; I didn't realise you were involved.'

'I was looking for a challenge, a chance to push the boundaries a bit, and I found it. I've been there four years and it's all been good.'

She nodded. 'I was wondering… Your mother…?'

'She's well. In full remission.'

Suddenly, Mimi's smile held nothing in reserve. 'I'm so glad to hear that.'

'Thank you. She and my father moved up to Scotland a few years ago, but I talk to her regularly. I'll tell her you were asking…'

She pressed her lips together, shaking her head. 'She probably doesn't even remember me. I'm just pleased to know she's okay.'

Rafe remembered what Toby had said and

looked her straight in the eye. His chest tightened suddenly, as if his body was instinctively trying to strangle the words that he was determined to say. 'What is it? What are you not saying?'

She took one controlled breath, as if she was trying to steady herself. 'The job you had, before Hartsholme. It fell through?'

'No. I was covering for someone on maternity leave. It lasted longer than I thought.'

'And your parents? They suddenly decided to up sticks and move?'

He could see the way this was going, but he couldn't stop it now. 'No. They'd planned to go when my father retired. The cancer delayed it a bit, but...'

She turned her back on him, planting her hands on the counter top, her head bowed. Something that sounded like a sob escaped her lips. 'Rafe... How could you...?'

This was a far cry to the indifference she'd shown when he'd left. Then, she'd accepted his reasons without question, but now she knew that they were excuses, given because he didn't know how to tell her the truth. The thought that maybe this was truly how she felt made him shiver with guilt.

When she faced him again her face was twisted into a mask of anger. Somehow that was worse than the tears he'd expected, because he knew now that her fury disguised an awful, unknown hurt.

'Get out.'

There was only one thing he could do. Only one thing to say.

'No.'

Mimi stared at him. Now was a fine time to suddenly decide he wanted to stay around. 'I said…'

'Yeah. I heard. Not until you listen to what I have to say.' His jaw was set in an immovable line.

'I don't want to hear it, Rafe.' She felt breathless, almost giddy with rage. 'I was never good enough for you, but you know what? I'm over it. This is *my* house, and *my* life. If you want to pick holes in it, then you can go and do it on your own time.'

'What…?' Shock registered on his face. 'What on earth do you mean, not good enough?'

'Don't pretend you don't know.' She'd vowed she wasn't going to do this, but it was all too much. The feelings were flooding out with as much force as the water that had separated her from Jack. 'I'm not a doctor, or a lawyer like your sister. My mum and dad didn't live in a big house, and I didn't go to private school.'

'You think I care…'

'Well, clearly you do. You didn't even let me try to help when your mother became ill; you just got in the car and went over there on your own.'

'But you had enough on your plate. Charlie…'

'Don't make my brother into an excuse, Rafe. You just shut me out. After all you did to help me cope when Charlie was injured…' She felt tears well in her eyes. 'How do you think it made me feel when you turned your back on me when I tried to help you?'

He didn't answer. Probably didn't *have* an answer, because he wouldn't have thought of that. In the silence she felt her heart begin to slow, and the burden of things left unsaid shifted slightly. Maybe she should have told him this before.

'It wasn't like that.' He was looking at her steadily but his hands were trembling. The thought that she'd finally goaded him into some kind of reaction was a bitter triumph because it was all too late now.

'Don't…' Suddenly her legs felt as if they were going to turn to jelly, and she leaned back against the counter top. 'You can rewrite history all you like, Rafe. Don't ask me to countersign the last page.'

'Fine. Now you listen to me.' He was on his feet now, pacing restlessly.

'No…I don't want to.' Now that the rush of anger was subsiding, the feeling of loss was tearing at her. Along with a horrible feeling that Rafe could talk her round if he really wanted to, because he'd always been able to.

He came to a halt opposite her. When she looked away, she felt his fingers brush her arm. 'Look at me.'

She didn't move.

'All right then. Just listen. I wanted to accept your help but I just didn't know how. I was brought up to cope, not talk. Never to talk, because that was a sign of weakness in a man.'

'All you had to do was ask, Rafe…' She looked up at him and the pain in his face silenced her.

'It's not that simple. My own father, the one who taught me how to behave, was failing my mother when she needed him most. He couldn't deal with not being able to make everything right for my mother, and he just shut down. I was doing the exact same thing. I was keeping everything bottled up inside, and I was failing you.'

'Why didn't you tell me?'

'It wouldn't have made any difference. And telling you…' He shook his head. 'Like I said. I was brought up to believe that talking about things was a sign of weakness.'

'And leaving fixed everything, did it?' In a strange way she supposed it had. When Rafe was around she'd filled the silences with her own fears and they'd thrived on that fertile ground. When he'd left she'd filled the void in her heart with ceaseless activity. She'd stopped measuring herself by what the men in her life thought of her and found ways to feel proud of herself.

'I think it did. Look at what you've achieved.'

'And… You? Your mother…?'

'I had to learn how to deal with things better and how to give my mother the support she needs. It wasn't easy, but I did it. My father…'

He turned away from her, flexing the tension out of his shoulders. 'He learned to text.'

'And...texting helps?'

'Yeah. When something's up he texts either me or my sister. Both of us if it's bad. We call Mum and she gets it off her chest, then she goes and tells Dad what she wants him to do.' He shrugged. 'Seems to work for them.'

'They're happy with that?' Somewhere, at the back of her mind, Mimi could hear an insistent voice. If Rafe's father could change, then why not him?

'Happy as clams.' He gave a wry laugh. 'Very understated clams. My dad's not all that different; we just found a way to work around it.'

He walked over to the stove, picking his coat up. 'I should go.'

'Wait.' She'd told him to go. She'd wanted him to go. But the haunted look in his eyes had changed her mind. 'You haven't finished your tea.'

'Thanks.' He put his coat back over the chair and sat down. 'There's one more thing...'

'No. Please, Rafe, no more...' She'd had enough

for one night. More than enough. She couldn't process it all yet.

'Okay.' He picked up his tea and sipped it. It was probably cold by now, but that seemed not to matter to him. Just being in the same room, without tearing chunks out of each other, felt calming.

'What did you...?' She pressed her lips together. She'd told him 'no more'.

'What?' He turned his blue eyes on her and suddenly the question seemed important.

'What were you thinking? Coming here tonight? Coming here at all, for that matter; you must have known we might bump into each other.'

'I knew how stretched the emergency services are here, and I really did just want to help. I reckoned on dealing with bumping into you if and when it happened. And tonight...' He shrugged. 'Perhaps it's only fair that if you're going to hate me, it's for what I did, not what I didn't do.'

Mimi was about to tell him that she *did* hate him, but something stopped her. Maybe she didn't after all. She turned away from him, pondering the question, and in the silence his phone started to buzz insistently.

She heard his quiet sigh of frustration. Then he picked the phone up from the table in front of him.

'Yeah… No, it's okay, I wasn't sleeping… Yeah, I'll go. Text me the details… Thanks.'

'What's up?'

'The house down by the lock. The fire brigade are in attendance and they've called for medical help.'

'I'll come with you.'

His gaze met hers and Mimi found the solid ground she'd been looking for. The place where they could work together, knowing that there was never going to be anything else between them.

'Okay. Thanks; it'll be good to have you along.'

He was trying to keep his attention on the road ahead, dark and glistening with rain. But Rafe could still see her. She'd been wearing a white cable-knit sweater and jeans. Trainers and blue spotted socks, with a blue ribbon twisted into her plait. A plaster wound around her middle finger from where she'd cut herself the day before. Every detail was burned into his memory.

He'd made her sit down at the kitchen table, and he'd told her that he was moving out...

'You're right. It's the best thing.' She'd agreed with him almost before he had been able to get the words out of his mouth.

'I'll just take my own things...' Something inside him had been screaming that this wasn't right, but she'd seemed so firm, so sure.

'Take whatever you want.' She'd shrugged as if none of it meant anything to her and then stood up, in a clear indication that the conversation was now at a close. *'I've got to pop over to see Charlie.'*

How could he have believed her? He should have known that her lack of emotion was just a front. But he'd struggled so agonisingly with this decision that the thought that Mimi didn't care whether he stayed or left was almost welcome. It assuaged the guilt.

When he'd packed his things, put his bags in the car and driven away, he'd thought he was being strong, protecting her. But now he knew the truth. He'd messed up, and he'd hurt her.

The thought that she still hadn't told him everything, that she'd given no reason for this crazy assertion that she wasn't good enough for him, wouldn't go away. But he'd already pushed her too far tonight.

'Wait... Is this right?'

Yes. It was right. They might have done it in the worst way possible, but it had unquestionably been the right thing to do.

Suddenly Rafe realised that she'd actually spoken the words and that she was referring to the fork in the road a couple of hundred yards behind them, not a decision made five years ago. Occupied with his thoughts, he'd instinctively taken the same road he'd taken then, which led on to the motorway.

'Ah... Yeah, of course. Lost my bearings for a moment.'

'Visibility's terrible. I nearly missed it.'

It was so easy to fall back into the pattern— Rafe driving, Mimi at his side, tactfully applying a corrective nudge from time to time. It made him feel strong to have her there, which was worrying in any number of ways.

He turned the car in the deserted road, driving back the way he'd come. It was still raining, and they still had a job to do. And Rafe was becoming increasingly certain that he couldn't leave until he found out what it was that Mimi had refused to tell him.

As he manoeuvred around a car parked right on the corner, he heard Mimi catch her breath.

'Oh, no!'

Water was pouring over the lock gates, spreading out in a huge pool on the other side. The lock house, converted now to make a holiday home for someone, was surrounded by three feet of water. A fire engine stood on solid ground, further up the hill.

'There's someone in there?' She was peering through the rain-drenched windscreen.

'Apparently. Must have been trapped and called for help.' Rafe drew up beside the fire engine and got out of the car. He identified himself to the senior firefighter and they shook hands.

'We can't get over there with ladders; they won't reach. We'll have to go by dinghy. We have information that someone's injured in there, but we don't know how badly.'

'Okay. We'll come with you.' He'd rather go alone, but leaving Mimi behind wasn't an option at the moment.

'Only one of you. Those guys are going and, with two of my men, that leaves only one place in the dinghy.' The firefighter jerked his thumb towards two men standing up close to the fire truck to get what shelter they could from the rain.

'Who are they?'

'Plain clothes police. The place is being burgled.'

'What?' Rafe hadn't been aware that Mimi was standing next to him until she spoke.

'Yeah. The alarms went off and the security company alerted the police. When they got here they found that the place was cut off and called us.'

'You think they're still there?' Mimi frowned, clearly taking stock of the situation.

'We know they are. The alarm system in the house is state-of-the-art—heat and pressure sensors, webcams, the lot. The ones downstairs are out, but upstairs they're still working. It looks as if there are two lads and one of them has suffered some sort of injury.'

'And the police are keeping a low profile not to spook them.' Rafe remembered the car, parked on the corner.

'Yeah. If they think that it's just the fire and ambulance services, then hopefully there'll be less chance of trouble. I'm sending over two of my men with the police officers, so that'll be enough to contain them if things get nasty.' The fire officer looked around at the activity going on behind him. 'We'll have the dinghy ready in ten minutes. Then we'll get you over there.'

'Thanks. We might wait in the car.'

'Yeah.' The firefighter looked up at the falling rain. 'Don't blame you.'

They walked back to the car in silence. Mimi got in, sitting quietly in the passenger seat.

'All right. I'll go.' Rafe decided to make his position clear, right from the start.

Mimi turned to him, no trace of the anger that he'd seen in her face more times than he could count today. 'This is my job, Rafe.'

He didn't care. Mimi was *not* going into a dark house which was in the process of being burgled. He didn't care if it was just kids, or that there was going to be backup. She wasn't going.

'Look, Mimi…' He heard the exasperation in his own tone and took a breath. 'In a situation like this, I'm handier with my fists than you are.'

'You're thinking of hitting the patient?' She was annoyingly calm.

'Don't be smart.'

She pressed her lips together, as if she was trying not to rise to the bait. 'Teamwork, right? You're a gifted doctor, Rafe, but I'm a first responder. I've been trained to work with the fire services and the police and I know exactly what to expect of them and what they're going to expect of me.'

Rafe grabbed the last and only argument he had. 'And, professionally speaking, a paramedic usually defers to a doctor in any medical situation.'

'Okay.' She sat back in her seat, folding her arms. 'Make the decision, then. From a professional standpoint.'

She'd pulled the last plank out from under him. Rafe had made some tough decisions in his life, but that didn't make this one any easier.

'All right. You should go. You're the one best qualified to do the job.'

'Thanks.' Her face suddenly softened. 'Don't worry.'

She went to get out of the car and Rafe caught

her arm. 'If you don't take care out there, so help me I'm reporting you...'

She grinned at him, irrepressible as ever. If this was all he could have, the camaraderie of working together in a potentially volatile situation, then he'd take it.

'You need to have a word with Jack. He usually threatens to string me up and flay me to within an inch of my life.'

'What you and Jack do on your own time is your own business.'

Mimi chuckled. 'I'd like to see him try.'

'Just go, before I change my mind. And be careful.'

'Yeah. I will.'

Rafe let go of her arm and she got out of the car, walking over to where the dinghy was being pushed out into the water. One of the firefighters helped her in and she sat down. Someone must have cracked a joke because Rafe saw a couple of the men laugh, and Mimi joined in.

He got out of the car and went to stand next to the senior fire officer, who was watching as the boat steered a path across the water. It drew up alongside a small balcony on the upper floor of the house, and two figures climbed up onto it. The crack of breaking glass sounded above the rush of the water and then the figures disappeared inside.

CHAPTER SIX

MIMI WATCHED FROM the boat as the two police officers gained entry into the house and were followed in by one of the firefighters. Glancing across the expanse of water, she could see Rafe, standing by the fire truck. Suddenly, she was glad that he was there.

The firefighter appeared and beckoned her inside. She knew that the place would have been searched and that it was now deemed secure. A hand reached down and she grasped it, struggling to find a foothold on the balcony, before an undignified shove from the firefighter in the boat behind her boosted her upwards.

'Through there. If we give the order to evacuate the house, you don't wait. We'll be getting everyone out.'

'Understood.' Mimi waited for her bag to be passed up and hurried through to the bedroom on the other side of the house.

The room was in darkness, apart from the light from torches and a lantern. A youth of about twenty lay on the double bed, groaning in pain. One of the policemen was with him and the other was guarding a younger boy, who sat on the floor in the corner of the room.

'He's got no weapons on him and I can't see any signs of blood either, apart from his fingers.' The policeman had obviously made some kind of preliminary check.

'Thanks.' Mimi climbed on to the bed. Looting was considered the lowest of the low, but this was a patient and he wasn't much more than a boy at that.

'Hi, I'm Mimi. I'm with the ambulance service.'

No answer. The lad's eyes were resolutely closed, although he seemed to be conscious.

'What's his name?' She turned quickly towards the boy in the corner, who had his face in his hands and seemed to be crying.

'His name.' The policeman standing over him bent towards the boy. 'Come on. You need to help your mate.'

'Terence Arthur Wolfe.' It seemed that now the

boy had decided to talk, he was going to tell all. 'We call him Wolfie.'

'Okay. Wolfie...?'

'Not now, baby. I'm not in the mood.'

She heard the firefighter who had come with her chuckle quietly and shot him a grin. 'Just as well. Neither am I.'

She tapped the side of Wolfie's face with her finger and he opened his eyes. 'Ambulance service, Wolfie. I'm here to help you.'

She started the basic checks, calling over her shoulder to the boy in the corner. 'What happened to him?'

'It wasn't my idea...' The boy started to sob.

'What happened, lad?' Another prompt from the policeman.

'He... He went downstairs, said there was stuff down there. I didn't go. All the furniture was floating about. He got hit by a wardrobe and it squashed him against the wall...'

'Did his head go under the water?' Mimi felt Wolfie's hair and it was dry.

'No.'

'Was he unconscious at any time?'

'I pulled him out and got him up here.'

'Has he been unconscious?' Mimi tried the question again.

'I don't think so.'

It looked as if Wolfie might have a cracked rib and two of his fingers were broken. But his breathing was okay, and if there was any bleeding it was internal. She turned to the firefighter. 'We'll need a carry cot. You have one on board?'

'Yep, we've got one.'

'Great.' She felt in her pocket for her phone and dialled Rafe's number. 'The boat can go back and fetch it?'

Rafe was holding his phone in his hand, and answered on the first ring. As he did so, he saw the boat, pushing away from the house and moving back towards them.

'Mimi?'

'I've got a young male, crushed by a floating wardrobe, of all things. We'll need to evacuate him by stretcher. I'll call an ambulance.'

'Okay, got it. I'm coming across with the boat. Anything you need?'

'No, I'm good. Thanks.'

By the time the boat arrived back, a carry cot

had been taken from the fire truck and they were ready to go. The dinghy was manoeuvred carefully across the dark water, bumping against the wall of the house, and Rafe waited for the go-ahead before he climbed up on to the balcony.

On his way through to the bedroom, a policeman led a young boy past him, ready to ferry him back to dry land and take him into custody. It seemed, from what Mimi had said, the other hadn't been so lucky.

She'd enlisted the help of one of the firefighters to hold a breathing mask to the boy's face and was kneeling on the bed next to him. A newfound respect for her bloomed in his heart. In this vital fifteen minutes she'd worked alone and by torchlight, improvising and taking the help she needed from whoever was there at the time. His responsibilities were different, heading a team of doctors and nurses in the hospital.

He'd been so close to making the wrong decision. Rafe had told himself that it was concern for Mimi's safety, but maybe he just hadn't respected her enough. He'd allowed himself to fall back into his old way of thinking—he was the man and he had to protect her. He did, but he had to protect her as an equal.

'Quite a few minor cuts and bruises, and pain in his upper left abdomen and shoulder. BP and heart rate are on the lower end of normal.'

'You're thinking a ruptured spleen?' Everything that Mimi had said pointed to that, but Rafe supposed she hadn't given her diagnosis out of deference to him.

'Yeah. I don't smell any alcohol on his breath, and his mate says he's not taken any drugs.' She twisted her mouth grimly. 'Not that he would have wanted to admit it, but the policeman made it very clear to him that he'd be in a lot more trouble than he is already if he didn't tell us. *Oof...*'

The air rushed from Mimi's lungs as her patient grabbed at her jacket, pulling her down on to the bed next to him.

'Gimme something, baby.'

Rafe and the firefighter both moved at the same time to release her from his grip, but Mimi had this under control too.

'Let go, Wolfie.' Her tone was suddenly commanding. 'I can't give you anything for the pain if you don't let me go.'

Wolfie let go and started to moan loudly, his hand moving to the left side of his chest, as Mimi moved clear of him.

'All right?' The firefighter moved his free hand to restrain Wolfie, and clamped the oxygen mask firmly back over his face.

Mimi grinned. 'Yes, thanks. He's surprisingly strong.'

'Okay, let's have a look.' Rafe got on to the bed and Mimi grabbed hold of Wolfie's flailing arm. A careful examination prompted howls of protest from Wolfie, the assertion that his pain levels were twelve out of ten, and a not so polite request for anaesthesia.

'I think you're right.' Rafe turned to Mimi. 'We'll keep him warm, continue the oxygen and monitor his BP and heart rate.'

She nodded as if that was an instruction.

'Agreed?'

'Oh.' She shot Rafe a surprised look but regained her composure immediately. 'Yes, agreed.'

'You're carrying morphine sulphate?'

'Yes and Naloxone.' Although it didn't appear that Wolfie had been taking narcotic drugs, the

Naloxone would reverse the effects of the morphine if necessary.

'Okay...'

She left Rafe to keep an eye on Wolfie and turned to fetch the morphine from her medical bag. When she offered him the syringe, Rafe shook his head.

'Your patient, Mimi.' He murmured the words. Now that she was a qualified paramedic, she was allowed to give a patient morphine.

Her grin felt like a reward, when he'd only given her what was her due. Rafe held Wolfie still, while she slid closer to him. 'Wolfie... Wolfie, listen to me. I'm going to give you something for your pain. Just lie still; you're getting what you want.'

Rafe felt the tension in Wolfie's body relax, and he started muttering. Mimi carefully swabbed his forearm, and when she slid the needle in Wolfie hardly noticed. She disposed of the syringe and then sat back on the bed, her hand on the side of Wolfie's face, soothing him while the drug took effect.

Rafe stood back, ready to step in if he was needed, but Mimi was handling everything correctly and efficiently. She managed to insert a cannula in Wolfie's arm which, given the bad lighting and the fact that Wolfie seemed to be trying to proposition her while she did it, was nothing short of miraculous. She was monitoring him carefully and the lad responded to the sound of her voice, lying quietly.

The firefighter who had been helping Mimi had gone to get an update on evacuating Wolfie from the house, and Rafe saw him appear in the doorway. 'How long before we can get him out of here?'

'Five minutes, maybe ten. We'll winch him down on to the dinghy and walk it over.'

Rafe had no clear idea of what that might involve, but Mimi seemed to and she nodded. 'We'll strap him into the carry cot as tight as we can. He seems a lot calmer now.'

'Hope he stays that way.' The firefighter winked at Mimi. 'Baby…'

She laughed. 'Wanna try calling me that when I don't have my hands full?'

'Nope.' He walked away, chuckling.

When everything was ready, Wolfie was carried through to the balcony and lowered down on to the dinghy. Men were standing, waist deep in water, on four sides of the craft, ready to guide it back to the waiting ambulance.

Mimi seemed about to climb over the balcony, to accompany the dinghy but Rafe lay his hand on her arm.

'My turn, this time.'

For a moment he thought she might argue with him, even though it was obvious that his height and strength made him the one for this particular job. Instead she nodded. 'Better take this.'

She pressed the EpiPen, containing the Naloxone, into his hand. It was highly unlikely that he'd need it now, but it was a kind of acceptance, that he was right.

'Thanks.' Rafe climbed over the balcony, wading through the freezing water towards the lights on the other side.

They'd handed Wolfie over to the ambulance crew, and Rafe had called the hospital to make sure that they were aware of the possibility that the incoming patient had a ruptured spleen. Then he'd made for the car, found a pair of sweatpants in his overnight bag and stripped off his soaked jeans in the cramped confines of the front seat.

The sky was beginning to show the first signs of an approaching dawn as Rafe drew up outside Mimi's cottage. Now that she had nothing to do, fatigue had taken over and she was already yawning. As soon as he got back to the hospital and into a hot shower, Rafe reckoned he'd be yawning too.

'What day is it?'

He had to think about the answer. 'Thursday.'

'Yeah. That's right, Thursday. I'm off duty for three days, now.'

'Right. Get some sleep.'

'I'll text Jack first...' She felt in her pocket for her phone and then seemed to give up, unequal to the task of finding it.

'If he's got any sense he'll be sleeping. Probably in a warm bed in the church hall.' A warm bed sounded like heaven at the moment but, however cold and tired Rafe was, he couldn't resist stretching these few moments out just a little.

'Suppose so.' Mimi stifled another yawn. 'What are you doing now?'

'I should get back to the hospital. Get a few hours' shut-eye and then back on the road.'

She thought for a moment. 'Why don't you stay here? You won't get any sleep in the doctor's on-call room today, and anyway you need to wash and dry your clothes. And you won't have to drive back out here to pick me up later on.'

'Pick you up? Where am I taking you?'

'I don't have a vehicle or a partner, remember?' A little quiver of her lip betrayed her uncertainty. 'If you still want me around, that is.'

He wanted her. 'Think you can put up with me?'

A tired grin. 'I'll try.' She opened the car door and started to climb wearily out. 'So are you coming...?'

Rafe reached for his overnight bag and pulled it out. Locking the car, he followed her up the front path and into the house.

Mimi fussed about a bit, leading the way into the spare room and switching on a lamp by the bed, which gave so little light that it served only to stop him from bumping into the furniture. She gathered a few items of washing that were drying by the window and then collapsed the drying rack.

'Leave your clothes in the basket in the bathroom and I'll put them in the washing machine tomorrow morning.'

Rafe nodded.

'I'll get you a towel...' She walked out of the room, reappearing a few moments later with a clean towel and putting it on the bed. 'Bathroom's all yours.'

'Thanks.'

'Have you...' She frowned as if she'd forgotten what she was about to say. 'Is there anything you need?'

'Go to bed.' He could have slept on a washing line at the moment, and Mimi looked as if she was half-asleep already.

'Yeah.' She swayed a little as she turned, and Rafe wondered whether he should follow her to make sure she got to her bedroom without falling asleep on the way. Then she left him, closing the door behind her.

Rafe waited until he heard the door of the main bedroom close and then walked the few steps across the hallway to the bathroom. He showered off the bits of river mud, revelling in the hot water, and then made his way back to the spare room.

He had neither the energy nor the inclination to worry about what he was doing here, or how awkward things might be when they woke. Rafe loosened the towel from around his waist and crawled into bed.

He woke slowly, knowing that he wasn't anywhere familiar but unable for the moment to work out exactly where he was. In fact he probably wasn't awake at all because he could smell the citrus scent of Mimi's favourite soap. Rafe considered the possibility of lucid dreaming and whether he could control what happened next. Then he opened his eyes.

Not bad for a first try. Mimi wasn't draped over the end of the bed, wearing black lace. On the other hand, the smell of cooking was wafting up from the kitchen. Bacon sandwiches would be his second choice of things he most wanted to wake up to at the moment.

He tried again and failed. He must be awake. Rafe stumbled out of bed and drew the curtains, looking up at the sky. It was iron-grey and threatening, but at least it wasn't raining.

Turning, he caught his breath. If none of the rest of Mimi's house held any memories, this room was full of them. The walls were a plain cream colour, and the pale blue patterned curtains and bedding were unfamiliar, but the bed was the sturdy pine one that he and Mimi had shared. And against the far wall was an old mahogany wash stand.

The memory hit him like a punch to the chest and Rafe wondered for a moment whether his heart had really stopped or it just felt that it had. They'd found the washstand in an auction, sitting unwanted in the corner and covered with grime. But Mimi had seen some virtue in it and so Rafe had put in a bid and secured it for her. When they'd got it home, she'd gone to work on it, carefully polishing up the wood to reveal an age-old patina, removing the brass handles and making them shine. It had sat in the corner of their bedroom, transformed from a piece of junk to something precious.

He supposed that Mimi's ruthless purge of the cottage had been tempered by practicality. Here in the spare room, she didn't have to look at the furniture all that often, and so the few things that reminded her of him which she hadn't wanted to throw away had been consigned to this room, where she could shut the door on them.

The bed, rumpled on one side only, filled him with an unexpected sadness. He'd told himself that he was over Mimi. That had been a mistake, but he could rectify it. Last night had given him hope that perhaps they both might find some closure.

He wondered briefly whether he should pull some clothes from his overnight bag to make the three strides across the hallway to the bathroom door, but the towel was large and thick and it was easier to just wrap it around his waist. From the mouth-watering smells coming from the kitchen, Mimi was downstairs cooking, anyway.

He opened the bedroom door at almost exactly the same time as hers opened. Rafe caught a glimpse of her startled face, her green ambulance uniform, and then the door closed with a loud slam.

'Sorry. You first...' Her voice came from behind the door.

Rafe called back a thank you, wondering how she could be in two places at once. This was nothing she hadn't seen before, more times than either of them could count. So why had her sudden startled look sent an electric pulse travelling across his bare shoulders? And why had she slammed the door with such agitated force?

He padded across the hallway, shut himself in the bathroom and locked the door, switching on the shower. Clearly he had some more thinking to do before he could work out what either he or Mimi really felt.

CHAPTER SEVEN

MIMI HAD WAITED until she heard the shower running and then gone downstairs to see how Charlie was doing with the breakfast and put away the shopping he'd brought for her. When she heard Rafe's footsteps again, and the door of the spare room close, she ventured up to the bathroom to empty the washing basket.

'Doing his washing, now?' Charlie raised an eyebrow.

'Oh, be quiet.' The thought had already occurred to Mimi and she was trying to ignore it. 'He's meant to be staying at the hospital and he can't get these washed there. And we don't have time to visit the laundrette...'

She pressed her lips closed. Charlie was grinning, holding his hands up in a gesture of surrender, and she was protesting far too much. Mimi dumped the pile of clothes on to the floor, almost glad that the nasty-smelling mud on the legs of Rafe's jeans was enough to overwhelm his scent.

Automatically, she felt in the pockets. A little loose change in one, and in the other… Held securely in his pocket by a clip, Mimi knew what it was before she even drew it out.

'What's that?' Charlie's question made her realise that she was staring at the watch, running her thumb slowly across the face of it.

'He must have taken his watch off last night, so it didn't get caught in anything.' It was an expensive watch, but that wasn't what made it special. It wasn't obvious at first sight but, when you looked more closely, an old silver sixpence was set in the centre of the dial, behind the hands.

The strap was different, and he'd obviously had the glass replaced because the scratches that she remembered were gone. But the sixpence was what mattered. Rafe had said that his grandfather had carried it in his pocket for years, and then had the watch made for his only grandson when he went to medical school, saying he'd had all the luck he could stand and he was passing it on now.

Something tugged at her heart. She'd seen Rafe take this watch off the nightstand every morning and put it on. Having grown up in a world where he was surrounded by things of material value, this was the only one he seemed to care all that much about. He must have been so tired last night that he'd forgotten that it was in his pocket.

'Still got his lucky watch, then.' Charlie chuckled. 'Good thing *that* didn't go into the washing machine.'

'Yeah.' Mimi put the watch down on the table. Even there, it seemed to be radiating some signal, activating memories that she'd rather not think about at the moment.

She stuffed the clothes into the washing machine and was fiddling with the dial when Rafe appeared at the kitchen door. Thankfully he was dressed now.

She could hardly look at him. His thick, dark blue shirt was open at the neck and tucked into jeans that fitted better than they had any right to. Mimi thought she recognised the brown leather belt, or one quite like it. Suddenly this was almost worse than seeing him half-naked. The shirt couldn't conceal his broad shoulders, and the jeans only accentuated his slim hips. And her treacherous memory was busy filling in the gaps, reminding her that she knew every inch of his body and that it had always been beautiful.

'Have you seen…?' He was clearly looking for something.

'On the table.'

'Ah… Thanks.'

Mimi turned her back on him, studying the instructions on the packet of washing powder as if this was the first time she'd ever washed clothes. She'd armed herself against all the obvious things, his smile, his scent, but she'd forgotten all about the watch and it had sneaked in under her defences. She'd deal with it, though. Just as long as she didn't have to see him put it on…

Charlie came to her rescue. 'Hey Rafe. Good night's sleep?'

'Yes, thanks. Much better than if I'd stayed at the hospital.' He seemed to want to explain his presence here.

'I imagine so. Sit down; breakfast's almost ready.'

The scrape of a chair and then a sudden laughing exclamation from Rafe. 'Really?'

Mimi turned and saw that Charlie had pulled

himself out of the wheelchair and was sitting on a high stool next to the cooker.

'Yeah, really. Took a bit of work.'

'I'll bet. Nice one.'

Rafe was grinning from ear to ear. The same grin that Mimi had worn for days when she'd seen Charlie wave away his physiotherapist's help, leaning heavily on the parallel bars for support as he took his first laborious steps. Now, standing and even walking a little was something he did many times a day.

Suddenly it seemed all wrong that Rafe had missed out on that. She could have at least sent him a text to let him know how well Charlie was doing. She could have, but she hadn't.

'Have you heard from Jack?' Rafe was leaning back in his chair, still smiling.

'Oh... Yes. He texted me. Holme's completely cut off at the moment, so he'll be staying there for the next twenty four hours at least.'

'Everything's okay with him, though?' Charlie interjected.

'He said so.' Jack hadn't gone into details about exactly what he was up to, and Mimi had been happy to take his lead. 'Apparently ambulance control told him the same as me—that they don't have a spare vehicle and he should take his days off. They'll sort something out for when we go back on shift.'

'And, in the meantime, you and Rafe are doing your thing.'

Shut up, Charlie. Mimi gave him a withering look and he ignored it and began to dole out the contents of the pans on to three plates. Like so many other weekends when the three of them had eaten together, only then it had been either Mimi or Rafe doing most of the cooking.

Now, Rafe was sitting back, watching. He knew as well as Mimi did that you only helped Charlie when asked.

'Come and get it, then.' Charlie had finished serving the food and Mimi went to collect the plates and transfer them to the table.

'This looks good.' It was a full English breakfast and Charlie had crammed as much as he could on to each plate. 'I'm starving.'

'Me too.' She heard Rafe behind her but didn't dare look round at him. His hand shot out of nowhere and suddenly he was shaking Charlie's hand. 'Really good to see you on your feet, mate.'

'Thanks.' Charlie shifted on the stool and Mimi got out from in between them, carrying two of the plates over to the table. When she looked around, she almost dropped them.

Charlie was on his feet and Rafe had him in a man hug. It wasn't so out of the ordinary for Charlie—he did that kind of thing all the time—but Rafe... All the same, there was no trace of stiffness or reluctance on his part.

'I'm sorry I wasn't there to see it.' The admission startled her even more. The old Rafe would have just sucked up his regret and walked away, never mentioning it.

Mimi put the plates down on the table. She was going to have to find a way of not watching Rafe's every move, hoping to find evidence that he'd changed. She was going to have to find a way of not caring, and do it quickly before he left again.

As expected, they didn't have to wait long before they had a call from the control centre. With eight hours sleep and a good meal inside her, Mimi felt a great deal better about that. Being able to see where they were going was no bad thing either.

As they moved closer to the flood area, large puddles had become lakes and the fields were now deep in water.

The car slowed and came to a halt. In front of them, a dip in the road was knee-deep in water for the next couple of hundred yards.

'Can we manage that?'

Rafe was surveying the path ahead of them. 'I'd rather not try if there's an alternative.'

Mimi nodded. The surface of the water was almost serene but that could be deceptive. The road underneath could be strewn with sharp rocks and potholes, any one of which had the potential to put them off the road.

'That looks a better bet.'

Rafe turned the car abruptly on to a track that wound upwards and Mimi saw a handwritten notice pinned to a tree: *Diversion and Manor Hotel.*

'Yep.' She clasped her hands tightly in her lap. The Manor Hotel's main driveway was three miles further along this road. If they could get up to the hotel from here and then drop back down again they'd avoid the flooded section of road.

She wondered if Rafe remembered. Because,

as the old stately house loomed on the horizon, she was having difficulty forgetting.

Date night. Although it had been more than five years ago now, it was suddenly fresh and clear in Mimi's memory, a treasure that had remained untouched and unchanged. Preserved in every detail, right down to the note she'd found on the kitchen table when she'd come home from work.

Going out tonight. Dress up.

By the time Rafe had arrived home she'd been almost ready. He'd showered and changed into a suit, and complimented her on her dress. Then he'd kissed her, refused to tell her where they were going, and led her to the car.

They'd driven here. It had been a summer's night and they'd dined on the patio, with flickering torches lending a sense of drama to a good meal. As dusk had begun to fall he'd dropped a room key into her hand…

'A four-poster!' The solid, dark wood structure had been big enough to close the curtains, shut the world out for a night and have Rafe entirely to herself. 'I've never slept in a four-poster before.'

'You want to sleep?' Rafe's wicked, seductive

smile had made it very clear that sleep wasn't on his agenda.

'Got a better idea?' she'd teased him.

'Much better…' He'd taken off his jacket and loosened his tie. Picking up a wooden chair from the corner of the room, he'd placed it carefully and sat down. Mimi had known just what he wanted. If she stood in front of him he would be able to see her back, reflected in the big mirror over the dressing table, which would give him a three-sixty-degree view when she unzipped her dress.

Undressing slowly, she'd revelled in his gaze, his murmurs of approval pricking at her senses like fingers running over her skin. Finally she'd shaken her hair free across her shoulders and advanced towards him, perching on his knee.

'What next? Since you seem to have a plan.' Whatever it was, she had really wanted to hear it.

'Call it a fantasy.' He'd nuzzled against her neck, running his hands across her body. 'You up for that?'

'Fantasy night…? Yes, I'm up for it.'

He'd had to help her unbutton his shirt because her hands had been shaking with anticipation.

When he was naked, his clothes flung in an untidy heap on the floor, he'd broken away from her kisses, moved the chair a few inches and sat down again, his legs stretched out in front of him.

'Come here, honey...'

He'd settled her on to his lap, astride his legs. She had been completely exposed to him, her back reflected in the mirror.

'You like what you see?'

'You know I do, Mimi. More than I can say.' Rafe had spread his hands possessively across her back. 'I want to see everything. Touch every part of you.'

She'd clung to him as his gentle hands did just that and she'd been blind to anything other than Rafe. When he'd lifted her, she'd reached to guide him inside, sighing with him as he'd lowered her back down.

'You like what you feel?' He'd whispered the words, his breath caressing her neck.

'I love what I feel.'

The heat had started to build. Locked in each other's gaze, breathing together, hearts beating together more and more urgently. His hands had found her hips, suddenly clamping firm, moving her in the urgent rhythm that her body craved.

'Rafe...I can't wait...'

'Then don't.'

He'd seemed intent on making her come as fast and as hard as he could, and she'd known that if he kept this up he would get exactly what he wanted.

'Just let go, honey...'

The fantasy vanished abruptly as Rafe jammed his foot on the brake and the car jolted to a halt. Four other cars were all trying to negotiate the forecourt of the hotel and the man standing outside, trying to direct the traffic, wasn't helping very much. Rafe wound down the window, exchanging good-natured hand signals, and the car that had shot out in front of them backed up.

She could still almost taste his kisses. The last time they'd been here together, she'd been thinking about them for days, but then she'd been basking in a rosy glow of satisfaction and now the memories just left her hanging.

'Sorry...' Rafe was looking at her, and Mimi realised she'd let out a gasp when the car had stopped and she'd been thrown forward against her seat belt.

'Okay. His fault; he was lucky you managed to miss him.' She tried to swallow down the languorous warmth that she heard in her voice.

'Getting a bit crowded around here...' He waved another car past and pulled on to the main driveway, which led back on to the road.

'Yeah.' Too many memories. Mimi wondered if Rafe could feel them, hovering in the air. It was impossible to tell; his face was impassive, his gaze trained on the route ahead.

He had been a wonderful lover. Tender, thoughtful, with enough raw passion that they'd lost themselves in each other. But now they'd both found their way again. It was just a pity they'd only been able to do that when they were apart.

The car turned back on to the main road, clear of the water that had blocked their path. 'What's the next call again?' It was better to keep her mind on the job. Better to stop re-examining old wounds and concentrate on moving forward.

'It's a Mrs Potter. The controllers couldn't get much sense out of her; all she would say was that her son might be unwell.'

'Might be?'

'We'll see.'

It turned out that Mrs Potter was panicking because she couldn't get in touch with her son on the phone. Rafe had swallowed the frustration that Mimi knew he must feel and spent a few minutes checking the number that she was calling. The addition of a zero at the beginning worked wonders and her son answered immediately, clearly in the best of health. They left her in the sitting room, talking animatedly on the phone, and let themselves out.

CHAPTER EIGHT

THREE MORE CALLS and Rafe had successfully managed to scrub the Manor Hotel from his mind. He was about to congratulate himself on that, and then realised that remembering to congratulate yourself on forgetting something was a contradiction in terms.

He could do with stretching his legs, and there were no more calls for them to respond to. 'Time to take a break?'

Mimi nodded. 'The park's only five minutes away.'

That was exactly what he had in mind. The nature park's picnic area was likely to be deserted and the trestle tables would be too wet to use, but there was a nice view. Maybe Mimi needed to stretch her legs too.

'Stop!'

Rafe heard Mimi rap out the word at the same time as he saw two small creatures ahead of them, standing in the middle of the road, and braked sharply. As he skidded to a halt, the pair didn't move.

'What the blazes…?' The tiny animals clearly weren't wild or they'd be long gone by now instead of regarding them solemnly. Wet and bedraggled, they seemed to be all eyes and shivering limbs and very little else.

'It's Tommy and Tallulah.'

'Who?'

'Tommy and Tallulah. They must have escaped from the petting zoo.' She reached for the passenger door, opening it slowly so as not to spook the animals.

'Where's the petting zoo?' Rafe didn't recollect a petting zoo in the area and he supposed it must be a new addition.

'Not far. Jack and I took Ellie there and she had a whale of a time.' Mimi started to walk slowly towards the animals and Rafe got out of the car.

'Ellie…?' Clearly a lot had been happening in the last five years and he needed to catch up.

'Oh, sorry. I didn't tell you, did I. Ellie is Jack's little girl. She'll be five at Christmas. She loves the petting zoo.'

Rafe tried to get his head around an arithmetical problem that seemed simple but obviously wasn't. 'Did I miss something? Jack wasn't even married...'

'No, he wasn't... Isn't... It's complicated. He didn't know about Ellie...' Mimi's attention was on the tiny creatures ahead of them. 'Come on, sweetie... Tallulah...' She advanced towards the closer of the pair, which regarded her steadily.

'What exactly are they?' They looked like tiny bundles of wet fur with little hooves and big eyes. Given the rather more pressing possibility that Mimi might be about to get bitten, Rafe decided to leave the question of Jack's love life until later.

'Miniature goats. Get with it, Rafe...'

'Okay. You take the white one and I'll get the one with the brown splodges.' Rafe eyed up his goat warily, wondering how fast a miniature goat could run.

Clearly Mimi was a better goat whisperer than he was. She walked right up to hers and bent down, picking it up carefully in her arms. 'There you go, Tallulah. What are you doing here, sweetie...?'

Tommy took one look at Rafe and turned, trotting along the road away from them. Rafe followed, and Tommy picked up the pace a little.

'Get him, Rafe.' Mimi chose that moment to shout an encouragement and Tommy took fright, trotting into the long grass at the side of the road.

How fast could a miniature goat run, anyway? Rafe walked up to the animal and made a lunge for it and it darted to one side, cantering towards a clump of trees. It was certainly agile enough.

He heard Mimi let out a cry of dismay behind him and ignored her. If he was going to be outwitted by a goat, he'd actually prefer that it didn't have to happen with an audience. 'All right, then, mate. It's just you and me...'

Apparently this was some kind of game. Tommy stood stock-still, waiting for Rafe to approach and then dashed for cover. Rafe might be a lot bigger, but Tommy had four legs and was quick on them. A final desperate lunge and Rafe tripped on a tree root, crashing down on to the wet leaves.

'All right. You win.' Rafe rolled over on to his back and Tommy approached. They regarded each other steadily and Rafe reached out towards him. Tommy nuzzled at his hand and then tried to climb up on to his chest.

Carefully, Rafe wrapped his arms around him. Tommy trained his innocent eyes on to him, and Rafe unzipped his jacket, allowing the small, shivering animal to nestle against his chest.

Gingerly he got to his feet. Tommy seemed quite happy where he was now and was trying to eat his sweater. Rafe climbed the bank, back up to the road, and saw Mimi, sitting in the front seat of the car, her head bent over Tallulah, who was lying in her lap, wrapped in Mimi's ambulance service jacket.

'Poor little thing; look…' Mimi was wearing a pair of surgical gloves and had *his* surgical scissors in her hand. She looked up at him and frowned. 'You've got wet leaves all over you.'

'Yes, I know. Spare me the details. What are you doing?'

'She's got a piece of plastic wrapped around her leg. Look, it's bleeding.' Two pairs of wide brown eyes were trained on him and Rafe frowned. This was an unfair advantage.

'You're not a vet, Mimi.'

'I know that. We're Good Samaritans.' She

snipped the tight plastic away from Tallulah's leg, exposing a red raw wound. 'There. That's better, isn't it, sweetie.' She bent down, allowing Tallulah to lick her cheek.

There was no point in telling her that it wasn't a good idea to allow random animals to lick your face, or to mention that the scissors would have to be sterilised now. He had another pair somewhere. 'All right, so where is this petting zoo, then?'

'Half a mile along that track.' Mimi pointed to a new road that branched off ahead of them, leading into the trees.

'Right. We'll get them back there as quickly as we can.' Rafe wasn't about to admit that the large eyes and little shivering bodies of the goats had made him wonder whether taking them back to his house was an option. He got into the car, depositing Tommy at Mimi's feet, where he nuzzled against her legs.

'Drive slowly. We don't want them flying around…'

No. Flying goats were the last thing he wanted. 'If we get a call…' If they got a call, he wasn't entirely sure what he was going to do. People before animals always, but Rafe was not sure that he could bring himself to dump Tommy and Tallulah.

'We won't.' Mimi hugged Tallulah close on her lap. 'It won't take us long.'

He drove slowly into a large paved area, surrounded by low buildings. A woman appeared from one of them, jogging out towards the car. When she saw Tallulah in Mimi's lap she smiled broadly.

'Thank you so much...you've brought her back.' She opened the car door and Tommy jumped out, nuzzling at her legs. 'And Tommy, too.'

Rafe couldn't help grinning at the little creatures' obvious joy at being back home. He'd meant to just drive away and leave them, but instead he got out of the car, opening the passenger door so that Mimi could carry Tallulah.

'Do you have to go yet?' The woman looked at the ambulance markings on Mimi's jacket, and Mimi looked up at him imploringly.

'Not for a minute. We're on a meal break.'

'Well, come inside and eat. I'll make some tea.' The woman smiled up at him. 'I'm so grateful you brought them back. The rain washed away some of the fences last night, and some of the animals escaped. We've tracked down all the others, but we couldn't find Tommy and Tallulah.'

'They didn't get too far.' Mimi followed the woman inside the building. 'But Tallulah has a wound on her leg, where she got caught in an old plastic bag.'

The woman gave a tut of disapproval. 'I wish that people would think before they leave those things lying around in the countryside. You wouldn't believe the number of animals that are injured by them one way or another.'

She led the way through to a room that was kitted out with examination benches, not so different from a hospital surgery, only generally speaking the hospital didn't have cages for its patients. A young man appeared, white coat and all, and set about examining the wound on Tallulah's leg.

Mimi showed no signs of wanting to leave just yet and Rafe picked up her jacket, brushing the inside down. There were a few wet patches but they would dry in the car. Something nuzzled at his legs and a plaintive bleat reached his ears.

Tommy had been towelled dry and looked even more appealing now. Big eyes and a fluffy brown and white coat. Rafe bent down to pet him.

'Oh, look. He likes you.' The woman set two cups of tea down on the counter and Mimi took one, thanking her.

'I think he likes my sweater, actually.' Tommy was busy trying to nibble at his sleeve.

'Yeah. Goats. They'll eat anything.' The woman bent down, nudging Tommy away from Rafe's arm, and he started to lick his hand.

'It's not much of a hole. You could darn that.' Mimi was sipping her tea, looking at him speculatively.

'Darn it?' He raised an eyebrow. The Mimi he knew couldn't sew on a button and, unless she'd fundamentally changed in the last five years, darning was way out of her skill set.

'I said *you* could darn it.' For a moment the old warmth flashed between them and Rafe found himself snagged in a tingling sensation, which reached all the way to his heart.

'It's an old sweater.' He stood up to collect his tea and Tommy followed him over to the counter.

'Be careful. He'll be wanting to go home with

you.' Mimi chuckled and he saw the smile that up till now she'd kept for her patients and for Tallulah. This time it was unmistakably his, and Rafe found himself luxuriating in it.

'He's a great little guy.' Rafe took a swig of his tea and bent down to stroke Tommy's head.

The vet looked up from his patient, smiling. 'Well, she's okay. Just a bit of a scrape and the skin's broken where she tried to untangle herself. All she did was manage to pull the plastic even tighter. It was acting as a tourniquet, so it's a good thing you got it off when you did.'

Mimi nodded. 'I'm glad she's all right. I bet you've had a lot of animals brought in here after the flooding.'

'Quite a few. Not so much domestic pets—people are keeping them inside mostly—but a lot of wild animals have been washed out of their homes by the floods. We've had birds, foxes, voles, you name it. Even a couple of grass snakes.'

'Really?'

'Yeah.' The vet pointed to a large, leaf-lined aquarium in a quiet corner of the room. At first glance there was nothing in it, but then Rafe saw something green coiled around one of the tree branches, which was propped against the glass. 'Take a look if you like. But don't get too close; they're very shy and you'll spook them.'

Rafe smiled as she approached the container warily, stopping a couple of feet away from it. 'I can see them...' Her voice was hushed with wonder. He wanted to walk over and fold her in his arms so they could watch the shy creatures together.

His phone rang. Mimi turned and the moment was gone.

Resisting the temptation to pull his phone from his pocket and stamp on it, he looked at the caller display. He shrugged and took the call, listening carefully to the instructions that the ambulance controller was reading out at the other end.

'Got to go?'

'Yep.' Rafe checked the text that had just arrived, confirming the name and address of their next call. 'Got to go.'

Men holding small fluffy animals with big eyes. *Rafe*, with his strong arms and gentle way, and a small fluffy animal with big eyes. It was a little too much to bear.

Maybe it was emptiness in her stomach causing that pang. More likely, it was the thought of Rafe's tenderness, and her own instinctive reaction. There was only one thing that could have struck any closer to her heart.

'Where are we headed?' Mimi tried to switch back into professional mode.

'One of the farms, out by the A375. Three-month-old baby.'

If Mimi had been alone, she would have screamed and buried her head in her hands. What was this? Did fate have some sort of grudge against her? If the sight of Tommy in Rafe's arms had pushed all her buttons, then a baby was going to be even worse.

'A baby?' She tried to keep her tone level. Maybe Rafe would decide that it wasn't medically necessary to pick the child up.

'Yep. Probably just colic, but we'll make sure.'

'Yes. Good to make sure.' He was going to pick it up, she just knew it. Maybe a baby throwing up all over him wouldn't be so mind-bendingly difficult to watch. Mimi wasn't at all sure that would be the case.

CHAPTER NINE

THE TRACK WHICH led to the farmhouse was submerged and the house itself surrounded by almost a foot of muddy water. Rafe parked on the road and got out of the car.

'Looks as if we're getting our feet wet.' Mimi surveyed the muddy, rippling water in front of them. Her wellingtons were in her car, which was still parked back at the hospital.

Rafe opened the back of the SUV and leaned in, pushing bags and boxes to one side and pulling out a pair of heavy-duty wellington boots. At least he'd be keeping dry. Perhaps she could roll her trouser legs up far enough to avoid the water.

'Want a lift?' Rafe was grinning broadly.

No. The idea of being carried around like a rag doll didn't much appeal to her. The idea of being carried around by Rafe... Mimi swallowed hard.

'Come on.' He'd obviously had second thoughts about teasing her, and was now trying to keep his face straight. Somehow that was worse. 'We've got more to do today, remember? There's no time to go home and change.'

And if she got wet, that was only going to get in the way of the job. It was a first principle. Stay safe, stay dry, because your ability to help others was compromised otherwise.

'All right. Thanks.' She kept her eyes fixed on the ground, feeling her muscles tense in stiff, silent protest. He tried to pick her up, but had to set her back down again.

'Hey. Loosen up, will you. You're going to need to bend your legs.'

'Yeah. Sorry.'

'One medical professional assisting another to the scene...' He muttered the words under his breath and Mimi wondered if he believed that any more than she did.

She laced her fingers together behind his neck and he picked her up. It was actually more like taking her in his arms, holding her close. Mimi hung on tight, squeezing her eyes shut and burying her face in his shoulder.

'That's better.' He started to walk, the sloshing sound of water accompanying his slow strides.

Mimi clung to him, trying to think of anything else. The shopping list for Charlie. The forms she had to fill in for her new job. That was just making things worse. Every time she went to the supermarket now, the stronger image was going to take hold and she was going to have to deal with remembering this moment.

He was walking carefully, testing each step, but a sudden eddy of water made him pause, instinctively holding her tighter. Mimi felt herself move against him, her cheek brushing his neck.

No, no, no... She felt her face redden in anguish. She hadn't done that, had she?

She had. Without thinking, and entirely by instinct, her lips had formed the shape of a kiss when she'd jolted against him. When he'd started walking again the kiss had been planted on his neck.

He hadn't felt it. He couldn't have. One quiet murmur of approbation told her that he had.

By the time they got to the farmhouse her cheeks were flaming. He leaned over the row of sandbags, protecting the small flower garden in front of the house, and let her down on the other side.

Maybe his hand was just travelling in that direction, in a movement of uncharacteristic awkwardness. But his fingers brushed against her cheek and Mimi looked up into his face.

The cocky grin she'd expected wasn't there. Instead, a look of silent pain and uncertainty. Had she been so caught up in her own feelings of rejection that she'd missed his unspoken feelings?

'Rafe, I'm...I'm sorry.'

'What for?' He glanced round at the farmhouse behind her. They had a job to do and right now the people inside were probably watching them.

'Whatever it is, it's all right.' He straightened up. 'You're standing in a puddle.'

'Oh. Thanks.' Mimi stepped to one side quickly.

'Got your phone?'

'Uh?' She felt automatically in the pocket of her trousers. 'Yes.'

'I'll go back to the car and get the bag. Have a quick look at the patient and call me if there's anything else I need to bring over.'

'Okay. Will do.' Mimi turned and saw that a woman was opening the front door of the farmhouse, smiling at her. She smiled in return, walking towards her without looking back at Rafe.

* * *

Mimi had wanted to keep going, but when she'd received a call from the ambulance controller saying they were no longer needed tonight Rafe had stopped her from arguing.

'She said they were managing, right? We need to pace ourselves; we both have another week's work ahead of us. Isn't there something you need to do?' Rafe couldn't think of a single thing that he wanted to do more than spend time with Mimi. Certainly not a meal, eaten alone, and a bed at the hospital. But he supposed that she might have a greater range of options.

'Not really...' She turned away from him and got into the car. As she did so her phone rang.

'Charlie?' Something seemed to be going on because she frowned. 'Yeah, okay; that's fine. I'll do it. Text me the address, will you?'

She turned to Rafe. 'I don't suppose you could give me a lift to the hospital, could you? I need to pick up my car.'

'Yes, of course. What's up?' Rafe had been planning on going back to the hospital. Last night had been an exception.

'Couple of friends of Charlie's. Their house is

in an area that's prone to flooding and he told them to come and stay with him if they needed to.'

'And they need to?'

'Yes. He's getting a room ready for them, and he wanted to know if I could go over there and pick them up. My car's got a much bigger boot than his.'

'They'll be bringing as much as they can with them, I imagine.'

'Yes.' She was squeezing her fingers together in what seemed like an agony of indecision. Rafe wondered whether she was also wiggling her toes.

'My SUV can fit a fair amount in. We could fetch your car, dump the medical gear back at yours and go together.'

'Would you? I…didn't want to ask… But if the house is flooded…'

Rafe started the engine. 'That's what we'll do then.'

Mimi could barely see his SUV in front of her on the road, it was raining so hard. It had taken almost an hour to get here, but she'd called Janet and Matthew to let them know that they were on their way. When Rafe pulled up outside the house, the door opened and Matthew ran out and knocked on the window of her car.

'Better bring your wellies, Mimi.'

'I've got them.' She slid over into the passenger seat and felt in the footwell for them, pulling them on over her socks. Mimi hadn't been about to lay herself open for a repetition of the carrying incident.

Rafe was already jogging towards the front door. Matthew led them through to the kitchen, where Janet was drying cups and plates and stacking them in a high cupboard.

It was evident that they hadn't got here too soon. Water was leaking in under the back door, sloshing around on the kitchen floor. Janet was shaking.

'Mimi, thank you so much for coming.' Janet put the tea cloth down and turned to Rafe. 'And...?'

'Rafe. It's a pleasure.'

'Thanks, both of you.' Matthew held out his hand and Rafe shook it. 'We've loaded our car up, but anything else you can bring along would be much appreciated.'

Rafe smiled—the smile he kept for emergencies, which showed both his readiness to take on any challenge and his utter certainty that things were going to work out fine in the end. 'I'll help you carry your things out to the cars.'

Janet seemed to be sizing Rafe up. 'Matthew… the cabinet…'

'It's too heavy, Jan; we tried it already…'

'But…' Janet lapsed into silence, picking the tea cloth up and folding it carefully. She was in shock, resorting to small tasks that were not going to make any difference so she didn't have to face the one big task ahead of her.

Mimi nudged Rafe. 'They've got a really nice china cabinet in the sitting room. Maybe you and Matthew could manage to get it upstairs?'

'Good idea.' Rafe strode out into the hallway, and Matthew followed.

'We really appreciate your help, Mimi.' Janet was looking around the kitchen abstractedly, as if to make sure that it was tidy before she received visitors.

'It's a pleasure.' Mimi took Janet's arm. 'Are

these boxes to go?' She pointed to the cardboard boxes on the kitchen table.

'Yes. Our tea service. It was a wedding present.' Janet's eyes filled with tears.

'Right then. We'll stow that carefully, in the front seat of my car.'

'Yes.' Janet didn't move. 'Thanks.'

She seemed to be paralysed, dreading what was coming next. Mimi picked up a waterproof jacket that was lying on the table next to Janet's handbag. 'This yours?'

'Yes. I got it in the sale.'

'Yeah? It's a lovely colour. Where did you get it?' Mimi gave Janet the jacket and she automatically put it on.

'The place down by the cinema in town. The one that does camping gear...'

'I'll have to pop in and see if they have anything that suits me. Yours is really nice.' Mimi picked up a box and put it in Janet's arms. 'Let's get started.'

Once Janet had something to do, she worked with a will. The necessities had already been packed into Matthew and Janet's car, and now some of their most precious items could be

brought along too, instead of leaving them upstairs and hoping for the best. After a bit of bumping and banging about on the stairs, Matthew and
Rafe got the cabinet from the sitting room safely
out of the water's reach and Matthew appeared
with a pretty wooden box in his arms.

Janet beamed with joy. 'My sewing box! Is
there room for it?'

'Of course. We've still got my car to load up.'
Rafe strode down the path after Matthew to open
the passenger door of the SUV so that the precious box could be placed carefully on the front
seat.

Then it was time to leave. Janet picked up her
handbag from the kitchen, took one last look
around and then they walked outside into the
pouring rain. Matthew locked the front door, as
if in some way that would keep the water out.

Matthew put his arm around his wife's shoulders. 'We'll be back before long, you'll see.'

'Yeah.' Janet smiled up at her husband.

'No looking back now, Jan. Come with me.'

Janet nodded and the couple walked to their car
together. When Mimi looked up at Rafe he was
watching them go.

'It's such a shame.' Suddenly the sadness of it all struck her. 'They're losing almost everything…'

'You think so?' He couldn't seem to tear his gaze from the couple, walking so close, as if they were in their own little bubble. 'Seems to me that they're taking everything that really matters with them.'

Rafe led the small procession of cars back to Charlie's house, parking outside, while Mimi backed her car into the sideway, ready to unload it. Charlie had obviously been looking out for them and the garage doors swung open, light flooding out.

'I thought we could stack everything in the garage and sort it all out tomorrow.'

'Thank you, Charlie.' Janet had a hug for him.

'My pleasure. Dinner's nearly ready. Jan, come and help me, eh?' He caught hold of Janet's hand.

'I'll be there in a minute. I want to bring my sewing box into the house…'

Rafe gave her his car keys and she skittered off through the rain to the SUV.

'Mimi, Rafe, you're joining us.' Charlie spun

his wheelchair round as if the matter was already settled, making for the door that led from the back of the garage into the house.

'I should really get going.' Matthew had followed Janet and they were alone suddenly in the open doorway of the garage.

'Do you have to? You could have a meal with us and stay with me.' When Mimi looked up at him, Rafe realised that he didn't *have* to do anything. But even though a meal in the hospital canteen and a disturbed night's sleep in one of the doctors' on-call rooms didn't appeal to him very much, it was infinitely preferable to the mess he might get himself into if he stayed.

'It's not a good idea, Mimi.' It really wasn't. Last night he'd gone to sleep not realising that he was in the same bed they'd made love in, but tonight it was doubtful whether he could ignore that.

'I hurt you, didn't I?'

'It wasn't your fault, Mimi.'

She tossed her head, her fair hair slipping from the collar of her jacket and streaming over her shoulders. He wanted to touch it so badly, to clear the damp strands from her face. He wanted to touch *her.*

'But still...'

Then he realised. He'd hidden his pain from her but she needed it, just the same as he needed hers. Just as he had wanted some small expression of regret that it was all over, so did she.

'Mimi...' He took a step closer, and they were almost touching. 'Leaving you tore my heart out. And yes, it hurt a lot and for a long time. But, looking back now, it was for the best.'

'You think so?' There was an edge to her voice, a hint of anger. The final refuge of the broken-hearted.

'Don't you?'

Her cheeks flushed. 'I've no idea, Rafe. Not a clue.'

She turned away from him before he had a chance to answer. Walking to her car, she hauled out the heaviest box, staggering a little under its weight, until Matthew rushed to help her.

'I'm hurting now...' Rafe walked to his car, murmuring the words under his breath, even now not able to say them out loud.

He unloaded the car, working steadily so that

he didn't have any chance to stop and think, let alone stop and talk. When he was done, he exchanged handshakes and hugs with Janet and Matthew and bade goodbye to Charlie, waving away all of his protests that he'd cooked far too much for four and that only five would do.

Then Mimi. She was hanging back, fidgeting in one corner of the garage.

'What time shall I pick you up tomorrow?'

'Eight would be fine. If you get any sleep.' She seemed determined to leave him in no doubt that he was being petty and that thought was unexpectedly warming.

'Eight it is. Make coffee.' He turned, walking away from her to the SUV.

'You'll need it. They tell me those mattresses in the on-call rooms are like boards.' She flung the words after him and Rafe hid a smile. It seemed that cold acceptance wasn't Mimi's style any more.

CHAPTER TEN

MIMI WAS ALMOST surprised when she saw Rafe's SUV draw up outside the cottage at eight sharp. She'd slept last night, but it was only a long day and a very full stomach that had facilitated that. This morning she'd woken early in a fever of uncertainty as to whether Rafe wouldn't decide that she was surplus to requirements and that he'd be much better off working alone today.

She'd drawn the curtains back carefully, leaving a small chink next to the wall so that she could watch for him without standing at the window. Aware that pulling them straight might produce a telltale curtain-twitch, she left them as they were and ran into the kitchen. It wouldn't do to let him know that she was anything less than one hundred per cent confident that he would come. Unless he didn't, in which case she'd decided to text him and tell him that she hadn't expected him anyway.

It seemed an age before the doorbell rang. She almost took up her position at the window again, wondering if he'd changed his mind and driven off. But he was there, on the doorstep. Unshaven and looking slightly the worse for wear, but a night at the hospital would do that to you.

'I'm just making breakfast. Care to join me?' She made the request seem as off-the-cuff as she could manage.

'Yeah. Thanks.'

He followed her into the kitchen, taking off his coat and putting his phone on the table. Mimi set two places, taking juice from the fridge and setting the coffee machine to brew. The croissants were warming in the oven, and she piled them on to a plate and set it on the table.

'Charlie bought them for me. He got me some shopping yesterday.' There was enough for two here, and Mimi didn't want to give the impression that she'd gone out of her way. In fact, she'd already been out this morning, catching the local bakery when it opened at seven.

Rafe nodded. 'They smell good. I couldn't face the canteen this morning; I was going to pick something up when we got on the road.'

'You can't work without a good breakfast.' Mimi wondered whether that sounded as if she was mollycoddling him. Whenever she wasn't working, she'd always sent him off in the morning with a good breakfast and a kiss.

'Neither can you.' He motioned her to sit. 'I'll get the coffee.'

Mimi sat down, watching as he walked over to the coffee machine. He had a kind of grace, an economy of movement that served to emphasise the gestures he did make. Unshaven suited him. Jeans and a sweater suited him. Everything suited Rafe.

'Aren't you going to ask me how I slept?' He was leaning against the countertop, his arms folded, his lips twitching in a half-smile.

'Do I need to?'

'Not really. Just thought you might like to make the point.'

'All right.' She couldn't help shooting him her most innocent look. 'Sleep well?'

'Nope. I've got an ache in my shoulders you wouldn't believe.'

Time was that she'd offer to massage them for him. But then time was that he wouldn't have even mentioned it, considering that any aches and pains were his to deal with. It was an odd form of sharing, but nonetheless a break in his stubborn self-sufficiency.

'I dare say it'll ease once you get moving.'

He turned back to the coffee, grinning. 'Dare say it will.'

It was a busy day again. A good day. As long as they both kept up the pace, working as hard as they could, not leaving room for anything else, they were able to slip into the kind of relationship they'd never enjoyed when they were sleeping together.

Although Rafe was the doctor on the team, he was standing back, letting her take the lead with their patients whenever possible. Mimi could feel her confidence growing, and she was beginning to live for his quiet nods of approval.

By four o'clock she was aching from long hours spent in the car and her head was buzzing with both exhilaration and fatigue. Rafe stopped by a coffee shop, overlooking a pretty village green. 'Time for coffee?'

'Definitely. I'll get it.'

By the time Mimi had queued, passed the time of day with a couple of people and returned to the car, he was gone. She could see him over the road, sitting on a bench under a tree which was usually three feet away from the banks of the river which snaked through the green space but was now on the water's edge.

'You've got something to explain to me?' When she sat down next to him and handed him his coffee, Mimi saw that he had a pad of paper balanced on his lap.

'Nope. We're on a break.' He gave her one of his most gorgeous smiles. The one that said the world could wait for a moment. This was Rafe's safety valve. Some people talked things out of their system, a couple of her colleagues had their own blogs, but Rafe seemed to have developed the capacity to just change gear, leave it all behind for a while and divert all of his attention to something else.

'So what *are* you doing?'

'I'm making a boat.' He tore a leaf from the pad and started folding.

Mimi put the coffee down on the bench between them. When talking about things just sent you round in circles, sometimes Rafe's solution was the better one. It was usually a great deal more fun.

'Give me a sheet, then.'

Rafe's boat turned out to be a complex, double-hulled affair which took more than one sheet of paper and sported a sail. Mimi stuck to a basic coracle shape, but she could make three in the time it took for Rafe to make his one.

They walked to the water's edge. Like a pair of kids with nothing else to do but mess around with paper boats. Mimi carefully placed her boats and, as the surface of the pond rippled in the breeze, two of them floated towards his.

'Watch out, Rafe, my pirates will be boarding you any minute…' She grinned up at him.

'No, they won't.' He picked up a stick, nudging his boat away from hers, and it began to drift slowly toward the centre of the pond. 'And anyway…'

He produced a wrap of paper from his pocket. 'What's that?'

'Duck food. My secret weapon.' He gave her a Machiavellian grin. 'Found it in the glove compartment.'

He'd been feeding the ducks without her. Of course he had. She couldn't have expected Rafe to go five years without taking time out to feed the ducks.

He tipped a measure into his hand, and then hers. Then threw some of the food into the water. 'Here they come…'

A large green and blue duck was making for the food, diving for it as it sank beneath the surface. Another well-aimed throw hit one of Mimi's coracles and the duck tipped it upside down in its eagerness to get at the food.

'Hey! Two can play at that game.' She aimed for Rafe's boat and it wobbled slightly on the water as the grains hit it. 'Come on…' She urged a smaller brown speckled duck on, which was paddling across the water towards it.

'No, no, no…' Rafe clapped one hand to his forehead as his boat lurched and relaxed as it righted itself. 'Yesss…'

They were both laughing. Rafe managed to lure another duck towards her second boat and it nudged its beak inside before lifting it out of the water entirely. The little brown duck was making his boat wobble dangerously, but somehow it survived the onslaught.

Mimi still had one boat left, caught amongst the roots of a tree. Picking up a fallen branch, she clambered across to nudge it out on to the water. Leaning out to free the boat, she felt herself begin to tip.

'Rafe…!' A knee-jerk reaction—screaming for him before she knew quite what she was doing. And, by the same instinct, he was there, pulling her back from the water's edge.

He didn't let go. Mimi dropped the stick, turning in his arms.

'Nearly…' He was holding her tight. In a sudden, controlled movement, he threatened to spin her backwards into the water, and then pulled her back again. Mimi clung to him.

'You wouldn't…'

'Is that a dare?'

She knew better than to dare Rafe, particularly when he was in this mood. He might not actually push her in, but he'd find some way of dangling her so close to the water that she'd be hanging on to him, begging him not to.

'No.' She tightened her grip on his jacket.

'Because a dare would be...' Something melted in his eyes. The reserve that had been keeping them both safe.

'Dangerous...' She whispered the word.

'Yeah. Very.' He didn't let go of her. And Mimi couldn't let go of him.

Getting wet was the least of her worries. Rafe had her in his arms and the look in his eyes... Suddenly nothing was impossible. A vision of their naked limbs, twisted languidly together, flashed into her imagination, making her heart pound.

He was so close. His lips a whisper away. If he kissed her... If he *didn't* kiss her, she was going to kiss him.

'Please... Let me go.' If he didn't move away now, she wasn't sure that she could. And kissing him would only open up old wounds, not heal them.

Wordlessly he moved back, holding on to her hand as she stepped away from the precipice. Steadying her when she almost tripped over a tree root.

'Ready to go back to work?' His gaze was thoughtful. Tender.

'Yes.'

He glanced over her shoulder and Mimi followed his gaze. There was no trace of the remaining boats, both of them having been scuppered by the ducks.

'What do you reckon?' He was searching in his pocket for something. 'A gaggle of ducks?'

She grinned. 'No, I think that's geese.' Rafe had changed gear again, turning away from the things that threatened to hurt them. But this time he seemed intent on bringing her with him, lightening her load.

Mimi picked up the empty coffee cups as Rafe tapped a search into his phone. 'A sabotage of ducks?'

He chuckled. 'Yeah. Actually, it's not as good as that. It's a paddling or a waddling. Depending on whether they're in or out of the water, presumably.'

Mimi strolled to the car with him as he laughed over the list of collective nouns he'd found on the Internet. A murder of crows. A parliament of owls.

It was time to go back to work.

* * *

This was going to be the last call of the day. If it hadn't been for the fact that each call meant that someone was in trouble then Mimi would have been sorry.

'They should be on the road, here somewhere.' She leaned forward, straining to see through the rain and the darkness. A light shone briefly and disappeared. Then describing an arc, up ahead of them.

'I see them.' Rafe slowed to a crawl in the teeming rain as the car headlights illuminated a figure standing in the middle of the road, signalling with a distress lantern. Another figure was sitting, hunched over, in the shelter of a tree by the side of the road, and a few yards further up a car was nose-down in the ditch.

The white rear number plates reflected in the glare of the headlights and Mimi saw that it was a European registration, with a D under a circle of stars to denote the country. 'What's that? German?'

'Yep. Hope they speak English.' Rafe stopped the car and got out, jogging towards the figure in the road, and Mimi followed.

It was a woman. She spoke a hurried sentence that Mimi didn't understand, and Rafe frowned in incomprehension.

'Wir werden ein Krankenwagen.'

The woman gave her an uncomprehending look and Mimi tried again, hoping that the woman might get her drift. If she didn't, then Mimi was going to have to call the translation service.

'Ich brauche einen Arzt.' She smiled, jerking her thumb towards Rafe, and the woman raised her eyebrows. 'Um… *Sprechen Sie Englisch?'*

'Ja... Yes, I speak English. *Danke.'* She caught Rafe's sleeve, pulling him towards the figure by the side of the road. 'My husband is hurt. Please can you help us?'

The woman's English was slightly accented, but seemed fluent enough. It was common to find that people under stress spoke first in their own language, and that calming them down would improve their English no end.

Mimi found the woman's hand and took it. 'The doctor is here and he will help your husband. Do you understand?'

'Yes… Yes, I understand.' The woman watched

as Rafe hurried over to the man by the side of the road.

'I need you to help us.'

'Yes. What can I do?' The woman looked frightened and stressed but she was keeping it under control.

'My name's Mimi. Yours?'

'Annaliese.'

'Okay, Annaliese. I want you to help translate for us. Can you do that?' If her husband was hurt, then it was important they hear everything he had to say.

'Yes, I can do it.'

'Good. Thank you.' Mimi led Annaliese over to where Rafe was kneeling in the mud next to the man. 'What is your husband's name?'

'Leo,' Rafe answered. He'd already got that far and it seemed that he'd also checked the man for any life-threatening injuries as well. 'He's been moving around but I'll put a neck brace on him anyway, and then I think it's best we get him over to the car.'

Annaliese translated quickly for her husband but he was already trying to get to his feet.

'All right...' Rafe laid a hand on his shoulder. 'Stay still for one minute. Let us help you.'

Mimi jogged back to the car to fetch the neck brace and, when Rafe had fastened it securely, they got him on to his feet. With one at each side to support him, they walked him slowly over to the SUV, sitting him in the back seat. He was wet through and shaking.

'It's ten minutes to the hospital.' Mimi looked at Rafe. She knew that he was weighing up all the factors. It was impossible to treat him effectively here, and the quickest way to get him warm was to go straight to A and E.

'Yeah. He seems alert and I can't find any signs of major injury.' Rafe considered the question for a brief moment. 'We'll take him now?'

'Yes, I agree. Would you like me to drive?'

'The steering's pretty heavy...' Rafe hesitated and then smiled, handing over his car keys. 'Why don't you drive? I'll sit in the back seat and keep an eye on him.'

Good call. If she could handle an ambulance, she could handle Rafe's SUV. 'Don't worry. I'll be gentle with your car.'

'You'd better be.'

* * *

The A and E department of the hospital was always busy, but tonight it was *busy*. The doctor in charge recognised Rafe, though, and after an exchanged greeting waved them through to an empty cubicle. It seemed that they were going to be keeping their patient for a little while longer.

Mimi sat Annaliese down in a chair in the corner and helped Rafe get Leo out of his soaking clothes. There was only a gown to dress him in, but Mimi found a couple of blankets and tucked them around him on the bed.

Rafe's quick nod told her that he could continue with the examination on his own and she turned her attention to Annaliese, who was crying quietly now.

'Let's get your coat off. You must be cold.'

Annaliese nodded gratefully, allowing Mimi to help her off with her coat and overtrousers. She was moving stiffly, her arms shaking.

'Are you hurt?' Mimi had already asked the question out on the road and Annaliese had said she was fine, but she didn't look all that good now.

'No. I am okay.' Annaliese was holding her arm.

'May I see your arm?' Annaliese nodded and

rolled her sleeve up to expose a livid red friction burn. 'That's from the airbag?'

'Yes. I think so.' Now that they had reached the safety of the hospital, Annaliese seemed about to break down. Mimi had seen that many times before. People's courage brought them through to the point where they knew that they and their loved ones were safe and then took a back seat, allowing them to cry.

'The doctor's examining Leo now.' She leaned towards Annaliese confidingly. 'He's the best.'

'I heard that...' Rafe murmured the words without taking his attention from what he was doing.

'So did I. Thank you.' Annaliese smiled and seemed to relax a little.

Mimi took off her own jacket and dropped it on the floor in the corner. She'd known that the tension between her and Rafe was unsettling for their patients and now it seemed that the warmth was making itself felt too.

She set about cleaning Annaliese's wound. 'When I first spoke to you, in German...'

'Ah. Yes.' A sense of fun suddenly showed in Annaliese's face.

'What did I say? You looked a bit puzzled.'

'You told me that you were turning into an ambulance.' Annaliese smiled. 'But I understood. You made a mistake that is common with English speakers.'

'What did I say afterwards?'

'You said that you needed a doctor.'

Mimi pulled an embarrassed face and heard Rafe chuckle quietly. 'At least you were somewhere in the ballpark.'

'*Ja...* Yes, it is good to try.' Annaliese turned to her husband, speaking quickly to him in German, and he nodded, managing a smile.

'I don't suppose you could write the correct wording down for me, could you? I meet a lot of different people in the course of my job and it might come in handy in the future.'

'Yes, of course. I have paper...' Annaliese reached for her handbag eagerly, and Mimi stopped her.

'We'll get your arm sorted out first. Then you can give me some lessons.'

Annaliese was wrapped in a blanket, sitting by the side of her husband's bed, sipping a hot drink. Mimi had ascertained that her clothes were wet only around the shoulders and fetched a spare T-shirt from her own locker, along with a blanket and a drink. Annaliese received the comb that Mimi handed her with a smile. It was the little things that did the most to reassure people sometimes. Taking the time to comb your hair was a step back into normality.

Rafe had concentrated on Leo. Now that he was warm and dry, and his distress levels were reduced, it became clear that his English was good enough for them to communicate directly, without needing a translator. His injuries were relatively minor but needed treatment and care—a broken wrist, shock and slight concussion, along with rapidly forming bruises on his face and chest.

Rafe beckoned to Mimi and she followed him out of the cubicle. 'I'm going to see if I can find a bed for him. I wouldn't normally admit him, but he needs care and rest. I assume they have nowhere to go?'

'No. Annaliese said that they left their hotel in Exeter to drive to one here, not realising that it was flooded. Apparently the hotel didn't think to phone people and let them know, just expected everyone not to come.'

'Great. Masterpiece of forward thinking.'

'Yeah. They were looking for other accommodation when their car went off the road.'

'So what are we going to do with her?' Rafe knew that the correct procedure was to alert hospital services and they would find somewhere for Annaliese but, from the snatches of conversation he'd heard between the two women, maybe Mimi had other ideas.

'I've called Charlie. With Jan and Matthew there, he can only offer her the sofa bed, but I reckon it's better than a mattress on the floor in a community centre somewhere. She'll never get a hotel tonight, and Charlie will be around tomorrow to get her to the hospital.'

'She's okay with that?'

'Yeah. Fine. Charlie's got room for Leo as well, if you want to release him.'

'I'd prefer he stays here, if they have a bed for him.'

She nodded, reaching into her pocket and pulling out a bunch of keys. Slipping a familiar one off the ring, she handed it to him. 'Here. I'll go on ahead with Annaliese and you can follow when you're finished.'

'Are you sure?' Rafe had resolved not to go back to Mimi's cottage again but, now that he had the key in his hand, temptation made him waver.

She hesitated, her cheeks flushing red. 'I'd like to talk to you.'

He couldn't say no now. Rafe nodded, pocketing the key.

CHAPTER ELEVEN

CHARLIE HAD BEEN ready with hot soup for Annaliese. Janet had fussed over her, going out of her way to make her welcome, and Mimi had left the four of them in the sitting room around a roaring fire, getting to know each other. She half wished that she could have stayed.

But her own quiet cottage was waiting for her. Rafe would be home soon. The thought twisted in her stomach. It wasn't his home any more. She'd erased almost every trace of him from the place, working in a fury of hurt and anger.

Maybe all the feverish effort had just been her own attempt to prove that she *was* good enough. And maybe she hadn't needed to after all. She opened the kitchen cupboard and, taking the bottle of emergency brandy out from the back of the top shelf, poured herself a measure.

Slipping off her heavy boots, she settled herself down on the sofa and swirled the amber liquid in the glass. No answers there, but it felt warm and relaxing. They couldn't change what they'd done, now. But perhaps there was some way that they could come to terms with it and get on with their lives. She reached for the TV remote and then threw it back on to the cushions beside her. She had too much going on inside her head to be able tolerate anything other than silence at the moment.

Her back ached and her limbs were heavy. Stretching out on the sofa, she sipped the brandy slowly…

'Hey…'

'Geroff…' She could feel someone's hand on her shoulder, gently shaking her. Mimi swatted it away and rolled over. The sound of breaking glass, and Rafe's sudden exclamation of surprise, brought her back to wakefulness.

'Careful…'

'Yeah, sorry. Didn't see the glass.' He was kneeling down next to her.

'That's okay. Have you cut yourself?' The glass must have fallen on to the floor when she fell asleep.

'Don't think so.' Rafe was collecting the larger pieces, picking them up gingerly between his finger and thumb.

'Well, you will do…' She huffed at him and sat up. 'Don't do that; I'll get a dustpan and brush.'

She stumbled into the kitchen, blinking when she switched the light on. On an afterthought, she collected up the brandy bottle and a couple more glasses from the cupboard on her way out.

'Have you taken to drink?' he teased.

'No, of course not.' That smile would drive her to drink if she wasn't careful. Or something far more dangerous.

'Watch out…' He frowned, and Mimi realised that she was about to tread on a piece of glass in just her socks. 'Sit down, I'll do it.'

He knelt down, collecting up the glass and brushing the shards out of the carpet, then disappeared for a moment to empty the dustpan into the bin. Mimi picked up the bottle of brandy, pouring a large measure into each glass. Tomorrow was the last of her days off, and so tonight might be the last opportunity she had of talking to Rafe. She had to make it count.

* * *

'I've been thinking about what you said.' She came right out with it as soon as he walked back into the sitting room, as if waiting might chip away at her resolve. That was typically Mimi and it had always made him smile.

'Okay.' He sat down beside her. 'What have you been thinking?'

'I think that I owe you an apology.'

She'd tried to apologise about something that afternoon, after he'd carried her across to the farmhouse, and Rafe had brushed it off. He was as mystified now as he'd been then.

'You have nothing to apologise for.'

She shook her head, brushing his objections away. 'You pushed me away, Rafe. That was your fault. But I was too afraid to ask why. I never tried to stop you from going.'

Rafe shook his head dumbly.

'And that must have looked a lot like a rejection to you.'

Emotion blocked his throat. The way it always had, and probably always would. Rafe took a sip of the brandy. 'Yeah. It did. But it doesn't matter... What I really want to know is why?'

She looked at him blankly. 'Why what?'

'Whatever gave you the idea that you weren't good enough?' She began to frown and Rafe stuck to his guns. 'I really need you to tell me.'

She took a mouthful of brandy. 'Okay. If you must know. The guy I went out with before you... After that friend of Charlie's...'

'The one you never used to talk about?'

'Yeah. Graham. He cheated on me. When I found out and confronted him, he said that he couldn't help it. He had a whole list of things I did wrong...'

'What? What things?' Maybe he shouldn't ask. But he couldn't believe that any of them were justified.

She turned to him, mortification sparking in her beautiful eyes. 'He said that I was boring. And that he couldn't help doing what he did because this other woman was dynamite in bed. Is that what you want to hear?'

Rafe stared at her. 'He said... Are you serious?'

She rolled her eyes. 'No, I joke about that kind of thing all of the time. Of *course* I'm serious.'

'It's rubbish. He's an idiot.' Rafe reached for her and she pushed him away.

'Don't. Just…don't.'

He couldn't believe that she could have taken something that was so obviously a cruel jibe to heart. Mimi was the most exciting woman he'd ever known, both in and out of bed, and this guy had to be certifiably insane. But she'd listened to him, and it had worked into her system like poison.

'Didn't *I* make you feel good enough?' Rafe knew the answer to that as soon as he'd asked the question. When she didn't answer, it confirmed everything. He'd never confided in her, and then he'd left, without giving any proper reason. He'd done nothing to repair the damage that had already been done.

She shook her head. 'It's… It doesn't matter.'

It *did* matter. Nothing he could say was going to make her believe how completely wrong all this was. Only one thing would do. Rafe leaned forward and kissed her.

She gave a little squeak of surprise and then she kissed him back. It was a proper kiss, not the brushing of lips against skin which hardly knew how to respond because it was all so brief.

They were both breathless, holding the kiss for

so long that Rafe felt almost giddy. He pulled her close in a sharp, strong motion and she gasped. Then she climbed on top of him, sitting on his lap, her legs folded on either side of his thighs.

This time he would tell her how irresistibly beautiful she was, how much she meant to him in every way. He'd make her understand...

She nuzzled against his neck and he felt her lips move against his ear. 'What's your number, Rafe?'

'You have it, don't you? Why...you want to call me?' Maybe this was some kind of complicated telephone sex game that Mimi had dreamed up. He couldn't help wishing it might be.

'No, idiot. How many girlfriends? Proper ones.' She nipped at his ear with her teeth and his whole body jerked with desire.

He knew just what she was asking. She didn't care about the ones who came before they'd lived together. Since then... He wanted to know who she'd been with since then too.

'Six. That's my number. And there's been no one since you...' Rafe decided that full disclosure was his only option. Her body was too close to his for anything else. 'No one serious, that is.

I've asked women to dinner or the theatre but that's all. The odd barbecue...'

She silenced him with a kiss. One that told him, without any doubt at all, that barbecues didn't count and six was the right answer.

'Three,' she whispered into his ear and he felt uncertainty tear at him. Two before him; he knew that. Maybe someone had helped her move the furniture and repaint the walls. 'Including you.'

An instinctive warmth spread through his whole body. No one since him. Rafe swallowed hard.

'And this tells us something?'

'I just wanted to know. Didn't you?'

'Yeah.'

She grabbed his wrists, forcing them back on to the cushions behind him. Then she kissed him again, somehow managing to tease and take both at the same time.

The anger, the new self-confidence which had been the source of so many arguments in the last few days, had translated into the physical. He'd always tried to be a considerate lover, and he knew that he could take them both into a state of dizzy satisfaction. But she didn't want that this time. *She* was going to take them there.

A sharp jolt of arousal spun through his veins. He stretched his legs out in front of him, longing for her to play out the fantasy.

She stilled suddenly, her lips a hair's breadth from his. 'Say my name. The way you used to.'

He knew just what she wanted. Rather than call her Miriam all the time, he'd simply stopped calling her anything. 'Mimi. Beautiful Mimi.' He felt his lips brush hers as he said the words.

'I want to know...' She was dropping kisses on his cheek, working her way across to his ear. 'I want to know how far I can take you.'

'Then find out, honey.' He wouldn't beg just yet. Not while he still had the choice. He had a feeling that Mimi might be depriving him of that quite soon.

'Be careful what you wish for.' One hand loosed its grip from his wrist and slid down to the buckle of his jeans. Rafe closed his eyes, feeling the scintillating fumble of her fingers.

'I know just what I'm wishing for.' Whether or not he was going to be able to stand it was another question.

She had the button on the waistband of his jeans open now and he couldn't wait. He just wanted to be inside her, to feel her taking him. Maybe she'd do it here. She could do it wherever she wanted and, when she'd had her way, he was going to take her upstairs and have his. She'd be coming underneath him, breaking apart so softly, so sweetly...

She seemed to know how much he wanted her. Her fingers trailed up his chest, finding their way to his face. 'You like this?'

'What do you think?'

'I think you do.' She kissed him again. He could taste the brandy on her mouth...

Brandy.

He didn't want to think about this right now, but the question cut through all of the sensations that were radiating from her touch. How much had she had? He couldn't remember, but he knew that she'd poured herself a large measure and that she'd been drinking while they were talking. Maybe it didn't matter...

It mattered. They'd had drunk sex before. Tired sex, no-time-for-it sex, practically every kind of sex in the book. But that was when they were living together.

And yet simply turning away from her now was unthinkable. Hadn't she just admitted to being the victim of one of the cruellest taunts possible, and hadn't he just told her that it wasn't true. If he remembered rightly, he'd kissed her to prove his point.

Okay. He could do this. He was quivering with molten desire, and Mimi was moving against him, but he could do it.

'Mimi. Wait… Wait…' He put as much gravitas into the words as he could muster.

'Rafe…?' Suddenly she was still, a look of uncertainty on her face. The realisation that this wasn't going to happen now, that he couldn't let it happen, almost broke him.

He cupped her face in his hand. 'How much have you had to drink, honey?'

Rafe felt her cheek burn hot under his fingers. Clearly she wasn't going to tell him, which wasn't a very good sign.

'Is this your idea of being…chivalrous?' She made the word sound as if chivalry was a deadly sin. Rafe dismissed the notion that if she could pronounce *chivalrous* she couldn't be that drunk.

'Would you get into a car right now?'

She shook her head. 'Probably not. But you never used to breathalyse me before taking me to bed. What's so different now?' Her body started moving against his. That sensual rhythm of hers that Rafe couldn't resist.

'The difference is that we've not been together for five years. If we really want to do this, then we need to make that decision with clear heads and in the cold light of day.'

'We won't, though, will we?' She was still again.

Loss seared through him. They both knew that this couldn't work. The only way he would ever get to touch her again was in a moment of madness like this one.

In that case he'd never get to touch her again. Rafe was *not* going to be the guy who took advantage of her when he knew that she'd had a few drinks. 'No. We probably won't.'

She nodded and climbed off him, getting to her feet and marching out of the door. 'You know, at this moment I could really slap you, Rafe.' She threw the words over her shoulder.

'You'd be doing me a favour...' He leaned back, covering his face with his hands. If she knocked his head off it would at least take his mind off his aching groin.

He heard her stomp upstairs, and then back down again. 'Don't even think about driving to-night; you've been drinking too. You can sleep on the sofa; it's a lot more comfortable than at the hospital.' Her voice was matter-of-fact, brooking no argument. 'And lock the door.'

He looked at her between his fingers. 'We don't need...' Maybe they did. He hadn't got around to thinking about what he'd just missed out on yet.

She dropped the duvet that was in her arms on to the floor. 'Lock the door. And, in case you're thinking about changing your mind, I'm locking mine too.' She turned, slamming the door closed behind her so hard that the key rattled.

He got to his feet, twisting the key in the lock, wondering if he should swallow it or throw it out of the window just to be on the safe side. Even when she was angry and he didn't much feel like it, Mimi still made him smile. He threw himself down on to the sofa, tipping half the brandy left in his glass away into Mimi's empty one and settled down to brood over the rest.

Mimi heard the click of the key turning in the lock. Almost overbalancing as she tiptoed back across the hallway, she sank silently to the floor outside the door, pressing her cheek against it. She wasn't used to drinking more than the odd glass of wine with a meal, and when she closed her eyes she felt dizzy. Perhaps she *was* a bit tipsy...

You started it, Rafe. She mouthed the words into the cool darkness. Maybe he had, but she hadn't exactly beaten him off. She'd been so turned on, and he'd been... She knew that he'd loved it too.

And in the morning a headache would have been the least of her worries. Mimi brushed her fingers lightly over the wood panelling of the door.

'Thank you.' She knew he wouldn't hear the whispered words. Slowly she got to her feet, her socks muffling the sound of her footsteps across the wooden floor in the hall. Then she climbed the stairs and fell fully clothed on to her bed.

CHAPTER TWELVE

RAFE OPENED HIS eyes and closed them again. Sunlight was spilling into the living room, and he felt as if he'd lost the use of his arms. When he tried to move, he realised that he was rolled tightly in the duvet.

Disentangling himself, he sat up. He was going to have to face Mimi. Somehow that seemed just as difficult as if he'd slept with her. But at least he could make sure he wasn't going to have to do it naked.

He picked his jeans up from the floor and stretched his cramped limbs. Unlocked the door, and then walked towards the sounds of activity coming from the kitchen.

She looked up from the coffee machine. 'You're up early.'

Rafe looked at his watch, frowning at the sixpence, which had clearly been falling down on the job lately. Seven o'clock. If he'd realised, he probably would have stayed put on the sofa for another half hour.

'Coffee?'

'Yeah. Thanks.' He eyed her suspiciously. She looked as bright as a daisy. Maybe he'd overestimated how much she'd had to drink last night. 'Do you have a headache?'

'No. I haven't got a headache.' She reached into the cupboard for a second mug, putting it on to the counter top with a clatter, as if to prove her point.

'Good.' Rafe sat down at the kitchen table and waited. This probably wasn't the time to tell her that it didn't matter if she was angry with him. Anger, any kind of emotion, in fact, was better than the way they'd parted the last time. And he was suddenly under no illusions. This *was* another parting.

She walked across to the table, setting a mug of coffee in front of him and sitting down. 'Last night...'

'It doesn't matter.' The words sprang to his lips by instinct and then he shook his head. 'Actually, it does.'

She took a deep breath. 'You were right, last

night, and I'm sorry. I was crazy to even con-
template…'

'I contemplated it too. And it would have been
a mistake, for both of us.'

He wanted to tell her that he *had* loved her, and
that maybe he still did, but that was no use because she deserved a lot more than Rafe knew
how to give. She deserved someone who could
share his feelings openly, who could heal her
wounds and make her see herself as Rafe saw
her. Beautiful, funny, talented… That was the
kind of list that she deserved.

Her gaze met his, and he realised that he wasn't
going to say any of those things. He didn't trust
himself, not after he'd so nearly made the wrong
decision last night. It was better to just leave it.

She rubbed her forehead with her fingers.
'Then we're done?'

'Are you okay about that?' There was nothing
else left to say.

She ignored the question, getting to her feet in
a sudden burst of energy. 'Why don't you go and
take a shower? I'll make some breakfast.'

It was an undisguised invitation to leave her
alone for a while. Rafe needed that time too. As

he stood in the shower, wondering whether being able to cry about it would make things any better, it occurred to him that this was the final confirmation that they'd made the right choice. Mimi was downstairs in the kitchen, probably crying into her coffee. And yet going to her was unthinkable, just as he knew that she wouldn't come to him. When neither of them could even do that, the best they could hope for was a civilised parting and a little closure.

Last night's rain had brought another round of injuries with it. Cuts, sprains, a dislocated finger, and a broken arm where a man had fallen out of a tree, trying to rescue a cat. At lunchtime they took advantage of a sudden lull in the stream of calls and parked up by the side of the road where groups of men were digging ditches, using the earth from them to make a barricade to contain the river on this side and protect the village which lay half a mile away.

Mimi watched as Rafe strode over to the men to speak to them. She didn't join him. It was better to let go a little now, before she had to do it for good this evening, and she was grateful for this opportunity to just relax back into her seat and close her eyes.

Last night had been a turning point. They'd come so close and then drawn back, acknowledging that sleeping together would be a huge mistake. She'd known it, but saying it made it real. She had to say goodbye to the fantasy that they might somehow pick up where they'd left off five years ago, and deal with the reality. She repeated the mantra that she'd developed over the morning. She and Rafe were no good for each other. He would break her heart just as surely now as he had then.

Someone knocked on the car window and she opened her eyes. One of the men who had been digging was standing there, his clothes spattered with mud and rain, his face creased in a smile. Mimi rolled the window down.

'Come and eat your lunch with me, miss.' He jerked his head towards a tarpaulin, strung beneath the branches of a tree.

It looked nice. A little patch of grass that hadn't been rained on steadily for the last two weeks. There were a couple of old deckchairs and a large metal barrel for a makeshift table.

'Thanks.' Mimi reached for the bag with the sandwiches and flask and opened the car door. In a gesture of old-world courtesy, the man held out his hand for her to take as she got out.

His bright blue eyes twinkled as he saw the size of her lunch bag. The cutting of sandwiches this morning had been more of a therapeutic effort than anything, and she had no idea how she and Rafe were going to eat them all.

'You need to sit down and eat a good lunch. Keeps you going.' The man was probably sixty if he was a day, but all the same he tucked her hand in the crook of his arm, in case she needed to lean on him on the way over to the tarpaulin.

It was a small act of kindness, magnified by the emptiness in her heart. 'You've got yourselves all set up here.'

'We've been digging along this stretch for days, all the men of the village in shifts. There's another gang down the road.'

'And no flooding so far?'

'Touch wood.' The man tapped his forehead.

'What about the other side?' The fields on the other side of the river were already deep in water.

'Can't do anything about the farm; Chris knows

that. We've done what we can to help him. My wife's up at the farmhouse at the moment, helping lay sandbags.' The man took off his cap and scratched his balding head. 'The water's got to go somewhere.'

'She's not overdoing it, I hope.'

The man chuckled. 'If you happen to be passing, you might just stop and tell her that; she doesn't listen to me. Now, you just sit down here.'

He brushed the dingy canvas of the most stable-looking deckchair and motioned her into it. Then he produced an impossibly clean white handkerchief from inside his jacket and spread it on top of the barrel.

'Thank you. This is nice.' The view over the river would look almost idyllic if she hadn't known that the bright reflections in the distance were the result of flooded villages and fields.

'Pleasure. Always a pleasure to see one of your people.' He nodded towards Mimi's bright ambulance service jacket. 'You're doing a fine job.'

'Thank you.' Tears were beginning to mist Mimi's eyes. She could just about handle the brittle good humour between herself and Rafe, the thought that after today she probably wouldn't see him again, but right now kindness was the only thing that could threaten to break her.

Rafe was still with the other men, clearly discussing earthworks, five heads turning one way and another in synchronisation as the men surveyed the digging. Mimi put her Thermos down on the handkerchief, hearing a dull clang as she did so.

'What's in the barrel?'

'That's from the brewery, miss.' The man tapped the side of his nose in a gesture of friendly conspiracy. 'Came floating down the river. We called them, but they've got enough to worry about at the moment.'

'The Old Brewery's flooded?' That didn't come as much of a surprise; it was right by the river.

'Three days ago. They're clearing out the mess now but I say it's too soon. There was more rain last night and the river's too high just now.'

'I'll bet you've seen a few floods...' This area was on a flood plain and the rivers broke their banks regularly every few years.

'This is the worst. Never seen nothing like this.' The man surveyed the expanse of water before them. 'Want a sip of beer with your lunch?'

'You're drinking it?' Mimi looked at the barrel more closely and saw a large shiny patch of metal where it had been cleaned and a tap inserted. 'It's been in the water.'

'You're telling a Somerset man how to drink his beer?'

'Well, no…' That would be sacrilege. And, anyway, Mimi knew that she'd be wasting her breath.

'Just be careful, though; that water's filthy. If I find you've made yourself ill I'll rat on you to the doctors and they'll be giving you every precautionary test that the hospital can throw at you.' If she had no jurisdiction in the question of beer-drinking, she could at least exert some authority on the matter of infection control.

The man chuckled. 'We gave the barrel a good wash before we tapped it. Made sure of that.'

Maybe she should get Rafe to enquire more closely on the matter. Or confiscate the barrel, or get the men to pour the beer away in the river. She glanced towards him. He was standing with his hands in his pockets, deep in conversation, obviously now a temporary member of the gang. He'd probably just clap the men on the back, congratulate them on their ingenuity and accept a pint from the barrel.

Mimi puffed out a breath and reached for her pack of sandwiches. For the next ten minutes she was off duty.

Rafe had strolled across and helped himself to a sandwich from the pile. 'These look good.'

She nodded. The coldness between them was already beginning to set in. When they were working and there was a shared objective, it was a little easier to ignore. 'Did you know they're drinking from there?' She pointed to the barrel.

'Really?' He inspected the tap. 'Looks as if they've cleaned it up...'

'All the same. I wouldn't take the chance on it...'

'Yeah, you're right. Leave it with me. I'll have a word.' He walked back over to the group of men, taking a large bite from his sandwich.

Ten minutes of welcome relaxation and then Rafe was back, jogging towards her, hastily putting his phone back into his jacket. 'Time to go.'

'What's up?' Mimi was on her feet instantly, grabbing her flask and the rest of the sandwiches and stuffing them into the bag. There was an urgency in Rafe's movements which meant only one thing.

'You know where the Old Brewery is?'

'Yeah, just follow the barrels floating down the river.' She threw the bag into the car and scrambled in. 'It's a couple of miles that way...'

Rafe started the SUV up with a jolt, spraying mud from the back wheels, and then they were on the road again, the group of men returning her hurried wave goodbye.

This call was going to need an ambulance in attendance, but they were nearby and every minute might count. A man working at the brewery had got careless and touched a live cable running from a generator.

'The ambulance controller told us not to move him. But the water's rising again...' The man who greeted them was obviously in authority here and he guided them quickly towards the red-brick building. The yard was awash with water and duckboards were laid across it.

'Where is he?' Mimi seemed concentrated on only one goal, striding towards the building. Rafe followed, carrying the holdall which contained the emergency resus gear.

He moved past her to lead the way, reckoning that since they were barely talking to each other she could hardly object. They went up a flight of steps, leaving the sludge-covered ground floor to find that the rooms upstairs were clean and dry, their white-painted walls seeming to defy the mess downstairs.

They were shown through to a large open area which smelled strongly of malt. A man was lying on the floor, a folded coat under his head. The small group of his fellow workers parted as they saw Rafe and Mimi.

Mimi was on her knees next to him. She looked down at the man and smiled. 'Hi there. Stay still now; the doctor's here.'

Rafe heaved a sigh of relief. He was obviously breathing and conscious. He dumped the bag and knelt down on the other side of the man. As he examined him, he heard Mimi questioning the men who were standing around, getting the information that he needed to know. The man hadn't been unconscious; he'd been thrown clear of the cable. His name was Grant.

'I'm going to clip something on to your finger now…' Rafe turned to fetch the pulse monitor and found that Mimi was already holding it.

'Thanks.' Rafe checked the small display and nodded in satisfaction. The man had some nasty burns on his arm and had cracked his head on the concrete floor when he fell, but he was breathing and his pulse was fast but steady.

The sound of running footsteps behind them, and a man's voice. 'Mr Harding… The water's rising fast…'

Everyone's head turned towards the man who had ushered Rafe and Mimi inside. 'How much time have we got?'

'Fifteen, twenty minutes. The water's building up at the back and it'll be coming in through the windows soon…'

Mr Harding turned to Rafe. 'We need to evacuate the building as soon as we can. The ground floor's about to be flooded again.'

Rafe turned to Mimi and she nodded in answer to his unasked question. 'Okay, we'll move him now.' He looked around for something that might be pressed into service as a makeshift stretcher.

'We've got a carry cot.' Mr Harding gestured towards a large canvas bag which lay on the floor.

'Really?' Mimi's eyebrows shot up and Mr Harding smiled grimly.

'Health and Safety. We don't take any chances.'

'Nice one.' Mimi was already unzipping the bag and taking out the tubular framework. The cot wasn't as sturdy as the ambulance issue ones, but it would do.

'I want everyone out of here. Pete and Stan, supervise that, will you?' Mr Harding gave the crisp order and no one moved. Clearly no one was going anywhere until they saw their work-mate safely down the stairs and out of the building.

Mimi snapped the carry cot framework open, testing its stability before she laid it next to Grant. 'You, and you...' She pointed to Mr Harding and another man. 'I'll need you to help us hold the cot steady and lift him on to it.'

She put everyone exactly where she wanted them, issuing directions to everyone. Grant was lifted carefully on to the carry cot and she tucked the pulse monitor alongside him.

'I need a coat...' Everyone immediately started

to take their coats off and Mimi smiled. 'Thanks, guys, just one. That'll do.' She took a light waterproof jacket and tied it over Grant, securing the sleeves together under the cot to augment the flimsy-looking straps.

'Ready?' Rafe had been keeping an eye on Grant, trying not to notice that Mimi was both unstoppable and magnificent when she swung into action.

'Yep. I want three volunteers to help with the stairs...' Mr Harding signalled to two burly men, who stepped forward with him. 'Right, now. This is what I want you to do.'

Under Mimi's direction, Rafe and the two volunteers manoeuvred Grant safely down the stairs. Dirty brown water was already sloshing around on the concrete at ground-floor level, and two ambulance men met them at the bottom of the stairs.

'We need to get a move on. Looks as if we don't have as much time as we thought...' Mr Harding was looking anxiously towards the back of the building, which faced the river.

'Okay.' Rafe allowed one of the ambulance men to take over his place at the carry cot and turned back up the stairs. 'You go on ahead; I'll fetch the medical bag.'

He took the stairs two at a time, glancing behind him when he got to the top to see Mimi, standing alone in the middle of the loading bay. 'What are you doing, Rafe? We need to get out...'

'I'll only be a minute. You go.'

'Forget the bag; we can collect it later...' She turned as an ominous groaning came from the back of the building, accompanied by the crash of metal hitting metal.

'Mimi. Go...' He shouted the words but she still hesitated, as if she was waiting for him. 'Now!'

She glanced at the stairs, then the entrance to the loading bay, obviously gauging which she should make a run for. Then she started to sprint towards the sunlight pouring through the entrance.

She didn't make it.

A loud crack sounded and a metal door at the far end of the loading bay flew off the wall, a great plume of water behind it. It travelled six feet and then crashed down, catching Mimi on the side of her head. Rafe heard her scream above the roar of the incoming flood, and then he lost sight of her.

'Mimi...' Her name tore from his throat in a ragged cry as he raced down the stairs. Pausing for one moment to try and locate her, he ripped off his jacket and plunged into the water.

Buffeted by the powerful force of the flood, he waded through waist-high water to the spot where he'd last seen her. Groping for her, almost blinded by mud, he plunged down into the water again and again. Choking and retching as dirty water found its way into his throat, he ducked under the torrent again. If he couldn't find her, then he too would be lost.

His hand touched something soft. He reached for it and found her arm, and tugged her towards him. Now that the water was reaching the same level as it had been at the back it was calmer and he managed to haul her lifeless body up into his arms. As he did so, a long shape disentangled itself from her leg and Rafe saw it borne away from them in the rush of water.

As he pulled her over his shoulder, it registered at the back of his mind. The dark brown body of the snake, with black zigzag markings. It looked like an adder, but he couldn't stop to find out. His first priority was to get Mimi out of here, and get her breathing.

He heard her choke, one feeble sign of life, and pushed doggedly forward towards the light coming in through the open shutters of the loading bay. Willing hands were there at the door, guiding him up to dry ground. Carefully, he laid her down on her side, on the bed of coats that had hurriedly been prepared for her.

'Mimi...' Rafe cleared her mouth and dirty water dribbled from her lips. Then she choked again, expelling the rest of the water from her lungs.

'That's right, honey. Breathe for me.' She had to breathe. If she didn't he would suffocate too.

She took one huge gasp of air and then her eyes snapped open suddenly, wide and frightened.

'All right. It's all right, Mimi, I've got you.'

Her hand moved unsteadily to the side of her face, where blood was trickling from a nasty gash. Rafe caught it in his.

'I see it. Just lie still for me, honey; you're going to be all right.'

She started to whimper, hanging on to his

hand. Mr Harding was kneeling down on the other side of her, watching anxiously, and Rafe spoke quickly to him. 'I think I saw an adder in the water. Tell everyone to be careful...'

Mr Harding nodded. The word was passed around the group of men behind them as Rafe wiped the blood from her face, hoping that none of it was the result of a bite.

Nothing. Just the cut, running along her jaw-line. Mimi was moaning fitfully and Mr Harding caught hold of her hand, talking to her and keeping her still. Rafe turned his attention to the leg of her trousers, which was ripped and soaked with blood.

There was a four-inch cut on her ankle, and blood was pumping from it. Above it, three double puncture marks, just below her knee. The snake, washed out of its home and terrified, had bitten her repeatedly, probably releasing its full supply of venom. Rafe pushed back the instinctive dread which clutched at his heart. No one had died from an adder bite in years.

'Mimi...?' A man's voice behind him. Rafe glanced round and saw one of the ambulance crew who had come for Grant.

'I need gloves, a dressing pad and a splint for her leg. We go in two minutes.' Rafe rapped out the words and the man nodded, turning.

'Rafe… Feel…sick.'

'I know. I want you to stay still, honey. Can you do that for me?' He wrapped his hand around hers.

'Yes. Stay still.' Somehow she managed a lop-sided smile. 'Hold on to me…'

'I'm here.' Her breathing was becoming increasingly laboured and she had started to wheeze. Her eyes fluttered closed and Rafe shouted for adrenaline.

CHAPTER THIRTEEN

THEY RAN ON sirens and flashing lights, Grant on one side of the ambulance, Mimi on the other. She had gone into anaphylactic shock, but prompt treatment with adrenaline had stabilised her. Rafe had splinted her leg to keep it still and now all he could do was watch and wait until they could get her to the hospital.

A team was waiting for them in A and E. Rafe followed the gurney in a daze, pushing past the nurse who caught his arm.

'I'm sorry…' He felt the nurse's grip on his arm, tighter now and more insistent, and he stopped, keeping his eyes on the retreating back of the doctor who was walking beside Mimi. 'But I have to go to her…'

'You have to step back now.' The nurse looked up at him, oozing no-nonsense sympathy. 'We need to get you clean and dry and then examine you.'

'I'm all right.'

'Maybe. But you're in the way here.' Rafe didn't move and the nurse leaned closer. 'Mimi's one of ours. We'll look after her.'

Rafe had called Charlie and they'd waited together in one of the family rooms. Finally the doctor who had been treating Mimi appeared, her face impassive.

Rafe had hung back, knowing he had little right to stand with Charlie and hear what the doctor had to say, but Charlie had beckoned him over. They listened together and Rafe numbly shook her hand, thanking her.

'Now tell me what all that means.' Charlie spun his wheelchair around, motioning Rafe to a chair opposite him.

'It means...' Rafe could hardly bear to think about it, but he knew that Charlie needed to know and he had to be strong for him. 'She's come through the worst of it. Mimi's very ill at the moment, but she's strong and fighting back. There's no reason why she can't make a full recovery.'

Charlie nodded. 'What is she facing now?'

'She went into anaphylactic shock when she

was bitten. That means they probably won't use any antivenom unless they absolutely have to, in case her body reacts by going into shock again. At the moment she's fighting back, but they'll need to keep a close eye on her. She's also inhaled a lot of dirty water, and that's irritated the lining of her lungs. That'll mend, but she's been admitted to the ICU and sedated. Rest and care are the best things for her right now.'

'What else…?'

'Everything else is relatively minor. She has some cuts, a lot of bruises and a fractured ankle. I missed it when I first examined her…' Rafe was still kicking himself for that.

Charlie rolled his eyes. 'Yeah, you missed it because you were busy saving her life.'

'I just did…' *What any doctor would do?* He hadn't. He'd felt close to many patients, battled for them with every ounce of his strength. But he'd always been able to maintain enough distance to keep himself sane. Never felt that his own fate was inextricably linked with the person whose life lay in his hands and that if they died he would too.

'How long will it take? Before she's up and around again.'

Rafe really didn't want to look that far ahead. He'd seen all the things that could go wrong in the course of his work, and he didn't want to think about any of them. But Charlie needed as much information and reassurance as Rafe could give.

'From what her doctor says, she'll be in the ICU for two, probably three days, if everything goes well. The inflammation on her lungs should resolve by itself in a few days...'

'And the snake bite?'

'It depends, Charlie. We need to wait and see. They won't transfer her down to the general ward until she's through the worst of it. But, after that, an adult can experience swelling and pain for up to nine months.'

'Nine months! But what about her new job?'

'I'll contact them and let them know what's happened. I can ask them to keep the post open for her but... To be honest with you, I think they'll be needing to fill the post before she's well enough to go back to work.'

Charlie shook his head, puffing out a breath. 'She so wanted that job.'

'Look, Charlie. At the moment, the best thing we can do is to take each day at a time. Looking ahead is just going to be overwhelming. She was treated promptly, she's being well cared for and her condition is stable. That counts for a lot.'

'Yeah, I understand.' Charlie reached forward, gripping Rafe's hand tightly. 'Thanks. When will they let us see her?'

'Soon. I'll go with you, and ask.' Rafe still knew enough people here and his word might carry some weight. At the very least, he could stay and explain what was happening to Charlie.

'Thanks. I appreciate that.'

It was the least that Rafe could do. If he hadn't gone back for the medical bag. If they hadn't been arguing about it… Overwhelming guilt gripped at his chest, leaving him breathless with remorse, and he tried to shake it off. That was for later. Right now he had to give Charlie as much support as he could.

'We'll go up there now and see what's happening, and then we'll go to the canteen for something to eat.'

'I can't eat, Rafe…'

'We'll do it anyway. The next couple of weeks are going to be hard, and you need to pace yourself.'

Charlie nodded. 'Just don't bring me chocolate.'

'You remember that?' Suddenly the years fell away and he was walking up to the ICU, a sandwich and a bar of chocolate in his pocket for the pretty ambulance driver who spent every waking hour sitting by her brother's bedside.

'I remember thinking it was just as well that someone was feeding her up. I had this idea that I'd sneak out when the nurses weren't looking, get to a phone and order up a pizza for her.'

Rafe nodded. 'Happens a lot. I've seen people who are seriously injured, and who think they just need a minute before they can get up and walk away.'

'I guess we all think we're indestructible.' Charlie's eyes were suddenly full of tears. 'Mimi always has…'

'She's going to come back to us, Charlie.' Rafe felt himself choke, and in a sudden terror wondered whether this was a response to the fact that Mimi too was choking. Maybe intubated. Frightened and unable to speak. He hoped that someone was holding her hand.

He *had* to stay calm.

'When you see her, I want you to remember this. She's going to look pretty bad. But I want you to remember that they're looking after her well, and that she's going to mend.'

Charlie took a deep breath. 'Thanks, mate. Got it.'

Visiting hours were over, but the ICU doctor had allowed them in for ten minutes. Mimi's body seemed very small in the bed, overwhelmed by the paraphernalia around her that was monitoring her and keeping her stable. Rafe breathed a sigh of relief when he saw that she was breathing on her own.

'Why is she in this room?' Charlie's brow creased.

'It's nothing to worry about. They'll put patients where they can best manage them; a separate room doesn't mean that she's any better or worse than anyone else.'

'Okay.' Charlie looked at the cannula in her arm. 'Is she in pain?'

'The drugs they're giving her will be enough to keep her comfortable.' Rafe looked at the label on the bag suspended above her head. He had every confidence in the people here, but he still couldn't help checking.

'Her toes...' Charlie was staring at the lightweight cast that encased her right foot. The other leg was hidden under a canopy, and Rafe dreaded to think what that looked like. Probably swollen, blistered and almost black by now.

'Her toes are just the way we want them to be.' He couldn't resist brushing them with his fingers, just to check that the cast wasn't too tight. The small, intimate act almost brought him to tears.

Looking at her face was an almost unbearable effort, but he made himself do it until the shock began to numb. One eye was bruised and closing fast, and a row of stitches ran along her jawline.

'I...I want her to wake up.' Charlie reached for Mimi's hand, taking it in his.

'I know. She's better asleep right now, mate. Just hold her hand and tell her you're here.'

'Will she hear me?'

'Maybe. Hopefully not, but tell her anyway.'

It was such an effort to stand back, watching

Charlie touch her and hold her hand. Hearing him say the words that Rafe wanted to say to Mimi. But he had no right to say them.

They'd eaten and then left the hospital. Charlie had given Rafe a lift back to the brewery to collect his car, and Rafe had followed him home. The lights of the bungalow were ablaze, and clearly Charlie's house guests weren't going to bed until he returned. Rafe nodded in satisfaction and accelerated on down the road, not looking at Mimi's house when he passed it. There was no way he was going to be anywhere other than the hospital tonight.

He dumped his overnight bag in the small cubicle that adjoined the duty doctors' rest room and lay down on the bed, fully clothed, trying to tell himself that he wasn't going to do what he was about to do. Then he gave up all pretence of sleep and went upstairs to the ICU.

He'd expected a gentle invitation to go and get some rest from the ICU staff. But the doctor on duty knew Rafe and beckoned him inside.

'She's very restless. I don't want to give her any more medication if I can help it.'

'What's she on now…?' Rafe held out his hand for the notes, knowing that he was pushing his luck.

'Just go and talk to her, see if you can calm her down.'

'Yeah. Of course…' Rafe followed the doctor to Mimi's room and walked inside.

In the muted light, he could see her hand twitching. Grasping for something. Maybe she was still back at the brewery, fighting to find something to hold on to, in the rush of water. The feeling that his heart was going to break, right there and then, hit Rafe.

'She's been like this for a while. She tried to pull the cannula out…'

Not good news. Rafe looked at Mimi's arm and saw that a bandage had been put over a new cannula insertion, to try and prevent her from getting to that one. 'Can I sit with her?'

'That would be good.'

Rafe pulled up a chair and sat down. Whoever Mimi was reaching for probably wasn't him, but that didn't matter. She was reaching for someone, and he could be anyone she wanted him to be if she'd just calm down and go to sleep.

He took her hand and felt her fingers curl around his. It was probably just an automatic reaction, but she seemed to relax a little.

'You're safe, Mimi. Nothing's going to hurt you.'

She lay still. He stood up, leaning over to brush a few strands of hair from her forehead. 'Go to sleep now. You're safe.'

Although her eyes were closed, he could see movement behind the lids as if she was dreaming. She was still fighting it, though. She moved in the bed and seemed to stiffen, as if in pain.

'Honey, please try not to move. You need to rest.'

Suddenly her eyes snapped open. They seemed unfocused and Rafe had no idea whether she could see him or not. But he repeated his reassurances, hoping that he was getting through to her.

She blinked twice. Then her lids drooped and she lay quiet. Rafe sat down beside the bed, holding her hand, feeling the tears course down his cheeks. This was the only place he needed to be tonight. Every night, until Mimi woke up again.

* * *

Three nights. Three nights when he'd been able to sit with her while she slept. Charlie had been there every day. Jack had come in, looking gaunt and tired, and been allowed to spend half an hour with her. But that was the daytime. At night Mimi was still his.

Rafe knew that he shouldn't be doing this. He was pushing his luck, asking more favours than he should, but he didn't care. He drove home for a couple of hours' sleep first thing every morning, and then back in the afternoon to speak to Charlie. If the ICU staff were willing to allow him to stay on and sit with her during the night, Rafe wasn't going to question it.

Mimi was improving. She'd been breathing for herself, her lungs recovering from the assault of the water. Each night she seemed to sleep more peacefully. On the third morning, as he tried to slip unnoticed out of the ICU, her doctor caught up with him. Eddie and Rafe were old colleagues and he had always made time to speak to Rafe when he visited.

'We're going to discontinue the sedative and

if she's still stable we'll transfer her on to one of the general wards.'

The small spot of light at the end of the tunnel suddenly turned into brilliance. 'Thanks...' Rafe tried to catch his breath. 'Thank you.'

'I'll get someone to call you. When she wakes up? Or are you going to get some shut-eye?'

In a world where Mimi was awake, Rafe doubted whether he could get any sleep. 'Thanks, but... Let her brother spend some time with her first. I'll wait.'

Eddie raised his eyebrows quizzically, but didn't ask. 'Okay. Just to let you know.'

'Thanks.' Rafe took the doctor's hand and shook it, gripping tight. 'You know when people tell you they don't know how to thank you?'

Eddie chuckled. 'Yeah, I know that one.'

'Well, trust me. They don't. I'm indebted to you...'

'Watch out. I might just collect.' Eddie turned and walked away, leaving Rafe to wander down to the canteen for breakfast in a daze of happiness.

'Thought I'd find you here...' Rafe was holding the paper in front of him, pretending to read it so that he didn't have to look at anything else. But Charlie's voice made him look up.

'You're early. Can I get you anything?'

'How can you eat at a time like this?' Charlie peered at Rafe's plate, where his untouched breakfast was beginning to congeal. 'Correction. How can you buy food and not eat it at a time like this?'

'Force of habit. Never let a meal break pass you by. They called you?'

'Yep. Said they were waking her up. The doctor said she might not be fully conscious until lunchtime.'

'Probably not. Everyone takes their own time.'

'I remember when I woke up in the ICU…' He saw Charlie's hand fist around the wheel of his chair.

'I know that was a very rough time for you, but you were badly injured, Charlie. It'll be a lot easier for Mimi. Remember that.'

Charlie took a breath. 'I will. Thanks.'

'She'll be drowsy, and she might well be uncomfortable. But this is a real step forward.' Charlie had been looking to him for advice and Rafe had been careful to keep his expectations realistic, but at the same time stay positive. He knew that Charlie's worst fears were grounded in his own experience.

'When should we go up, then?'

'I reckon an hour or so. They'll let you in early if they're waking her.'

Charlie narrowed his eyes. 'What's with the *you*? You're not coming?'

'She's…' Rafe shrugged. 'It's you she wants to see, mate.'

'Right. You two were arguing, weren't you?'

'Yeah.' Every time Rafe thought about it, it was as if a knife had been slid into his heart.

'More than you were when you first turned up?' Charlie grinned.

'A lot less than that, actually. In fact we were in complete agreement…' In the last three days the dogged determination that she was going to get better had overwhelmed everything else. But now… The sadness that Rafe had felt on their last morning together, when they'd both known it was over but hadn't been able to say the words, washed back over him.

She was waking up. And he had to go.

'You and Mimi broke up again, didn't you?' Charlie's voice was heavy with resignation.

'Well…we were never together, so it follows that we couldn't have…'

'Oh, for crying out loud. So you were never together, which is none of my business anyway, but you still managed to break up. Only you and Mimi could do that.'

'It's complicated.'

'Yeah, I don't doubt that for a minute.' Charlie was squeezing the bridge of his nose between his thumb and finger. 'But I'd really appreciate it if you'd wait with me. I need some company…'

Charlie seemed suddenly on edge. As close to panic as Rafe had seen him since the difficult days when he'd had to come to terms with the fact that he wouldn't walk again. This was the one thing that Rafe had feared, and the only thing that could persuade him to stay.

'I'll stay for as long as you want. She'll be okay, you'll see.'

'Yeah.' Charlie took a deep breath. 'I know. Thanks.'

'Let's have some coffee. There's plenty of time, and I could do with a cup.' Rafe's limbs were aching with fatigue, but the thought of a few more precious moments with Mimi made sleeping out of the question. Just as long as he left before she woke.

CHAPTER FOURTEEN

THEY SAT AT Mimi's bedside as she slept. Charlie had moved from his wheelchair to the perching stool which he had brought from home, the extra height allowing him to lean over and see Mimi's face, but after half an hour Rafe persuaded him to sit back down again and save his strength for when she was awake.

They talked, one on each side of the bed. Speaking quietly about the weather, how it had stopped raining. The wheelchair basketball league, the best beer gardens. Anything and everything, so that she might hear their voices.

'So some of us were thinking we'd have the basketball club crest tattooed on our arms. Only we don't actually have a club crest, so we'd have to get one first. And no one can agree on what to have...'

'Don't do that.'

Charlie suddenly fell silent. Mimi's voice had

been quiet but clear, and when Rafe glanced at her she seemed to be sleeping still. Charlie rapidly hoisted himself to his feet, twisting urgently towards the perching stool, but he slipped and ended up on the floor.

Now was no time to stand back and let Charlie deal with it. Rafe rounded the bed, keeping his gaze on Mimi's face, and offered his hand. Charlie gripped hold of him, swinging himself up and finding the stool.

'Mimi. No tattoos, I promise. Just wake up… Please…' Charlie leaned over her, his knuckles white on the bed's safety rails.

She lay unresponsive. This was agony.

'She might be like this for a while, Charlie. It's quite…' Rafe stopped short as Mimi's eyelids fluttered. They'd done this before and she'd drifted back to sleep. But this time…

She opened her eyes.

Tears spilled suddenly from Charlie's eyes and he lifted Mimi's hand to his lips. Mimi blinked a couple of times and licked her lips.

'Dry… Rafe…'

Rafe had told himself that he would leave as soon as Mimi showed any signs of waking, and let Charlie have this moment, but when he heard her say his name he couldn't help it. He leaned over the bed, careful not to obscure her view of her brother.

'Mimi...? Welcome back, honey. You want some water?'

'Yes... Tell Charlie...'

'You can tell him yourself. He's right here.' Rafe turned, brushing away his own tears as he reached for the beaker of water.

'No tattoos. I promise...' Charlie was babbling almost incoherently on the other side of the bed, and Mimi batted her hand as if to shut him up. Rafe dipped a swab into the water, holding it against the side of her mouth.

'Good... More...'

Rafe handed the water to Charlie. 'Careful. Don't let her drink just yet. A drop of water on the swab, just to moisten her lips.'

'Yes. Thanks, mate.' Rafe watched as Charlie carefully brushed the swab against Mimi's lips.

'My legs... Can't move...' She moaned, shifting restlessly in the bed, and Rafe stroked the side of her face to quiet her, the way he'd done so many times in the last three nights.

'You have a fractured ankle and it's in plaster. But it'll mend.'

'Snake…'

Rafe exchanged a glance with Charlie. He hadn't realised that Mimi had known about the snake. An image of her, underwater and alone, struggling for air and feeling the snake coil around her leg and bite her…

'I know. That's all been dealt with. You're in the hospital and you're safe, Mimi. No snakes here.' He wondered whether he should make the point by checking under the bed, but Mimi's eyes were closed now and she wouldn't see him. The thought that she'd faced terrors in her sleep made him want to wade into her dreams and protect her from whatever her unconscious mind could throw at her.

She seemed to calm, drifting somewhere between awake and asleep. Then she moaned again, her eyelids fluttering.

'Got to go to work…'

Charlie looked helplessly at Rafe. 'What's the matter with her?' He mouthed the words silently.

'She's okay, just a bit confused. You were just

the same when you woke up.' Rafe smiled reassuringly.

'Was I?' Charlie shook his head. 'I don't remember that...'

'What's the time? Got to go...' Mimi's eyes were still closed but she was trying to raise her head from the pillow.

'It's your day off. No work today. Just rest.' Rafe took hold of her reaching hand and she quietened again.

'Good. Tired...'

Charlie leaned over the bed, his shaking fingers brushing her cheek the way Rafe's had earlier. He seemed to be getting the idea of what he needed to do now. 'You can go back to sleep for a while, Mimi. Just rest. We'll be here when you wake up again.'

She heaved a sigh and then lay still again, drifting away from them, back to sleep. They watched her for almost an hour as she slept peacefully. Rafe knew she'd be waking again soon, and that this time she'd be more lucid. And he knew what he had to do.

Slipping his watch off his wrist, he looked at it

one last time and smiled. Then he held it out to Charlie. 'Give her this.'

Charlie stared at him. 'You're going, aren't you?'

'I'll be downstairs.'

'But… Don't you want…?'

More than anything. He wanted to see Mimi wake up, hold her hand and talk to her. 'I think… it's time for me to take a back seat, Charlie. Mimi and I made our decision, and it's best if I don't hang around now.'

Charlie seemed to be turning it over in his mind. Then he took the watch, his thumb grazing the glass over the lucky sixpence. 'I'll make sure this gets back to you…'

'No, I…' Giving something that Mimi knew was precious to him was the only way that Rafe knew of showing that he did care. That he hadn't just walked away, the way he'd done the last time.

'She should keep it; it'll bring her luck.' Rafe forced a grin. 'And she'll be able to check the time when she wakes up and thinks she needs to go to work.'

'Okay. I'll give it to her. You'll be in the canteen?'

'Yeah. Come down and let me know how she's doing? I'll wait.'

'Sure. I'll be down later.'

Charlie had found him in the canteen and Rafe had listened, greedily absorbing every detail of how Mimi had woken again and what she'd said. Rafe had extracted a promise from him, to call if there was anything he could do, and walked to Charlie's car with him, dangling his own car keys in a vain attempt to convince himself that he too was going to get into his car and drive away.

He'd told himself that he would just go up and check with the doctor on her progress. That she'd be sleeping now, and that if he looked in on her one last time she'd never know.

The doctor had told him that they'd tried to take the watch from her, but that Mimi had protested so fiercely that he had relented. The watch had been carefully folded inside an elastic bandage, and she had been allowed to keep it on her wrist. Drawn in, he sat beside her bed, watching her sleep.

'Rafe...?' He'd been staring at her wrist, wondering if the watch was too heavy for her to wear it like that, and he hadn't seen her eyelids open. But in the half-light he could see her gaze now, fixed on him.

'Everything's okay, Mimi. Go back to sleep.'

Her lips twitched into a smile. 'Again? That's all you ever say to me...'

She'd heard him. Those long nights when he'd wondered if she knew he was there. Rafe blinked back the tears.

'I'm thirsty...'

'Okay.' He operated the controls to raise the head of the bed. Then he poured some water into a glass, letting her take some water through a straw. 'Better?'

'Thanks. That's good.' Her fingers found the elastic bandage around her wrist, plucking at it. 'I'll take good care of this.'

He'd wondered whether she would try to give it back to him. The fact that she didn't, that she wanted to keep it, made his heart swell with happiness.

'It's supposed to be taking care of you. When it comes to good luck, you can't beat a sixpence.'

'No. You can't.' Her eyelids fluttered and Rafe

thought they were closing, but then she shifted in the bed, turning her head to look at him. 'You should go home. Get some sleep.'

'I will. In a minute.' When she was asleep. It hurt to even think about getting up and walking away and although there were many things he wished he could share with Mimi, the pain of parting wasn't one of them.

'Thank you for staying, Rafe. I would have been...so lonely...'

He brushed the tear from her cheek, forcing a smile. 'I was at a loose end...'

'Yeah. Me too.' She became suddenly agitated. 'You should go now. I want you to go home...'

This was the one thing that Rafe had hoped to avoid. He took her hand, soothing her. 'It's okay, I know. We made a decision and I'm honouring that.'

'Thank you.' She yawned, clapping her hand over her mouth. 'Didn't mean to do that...'

Rafe chuckled despite himself. 'I know you didn't. One thing before you go back to sleep. I want you to call me if you need me. Any time. Will you promise?'

'I can't...' She furrowed her brow, as if she was trying to remember why. 'My phone...'

Rafe turned, sliding open the drawer which held her personal bits and pieces. Her phone was inside, but smashed so badly that it was practically broken in half.

'Your phone's broken. So you'll have to get Charlie to call if you need me. Will you do that?'

She nodded. 'Promise.'

'Good. Go to sleep now, Mimi.'

'Yes. I'm...tired.'

She yawned again, and then seemed to settle. Rafe waited. He'd seen enough people pretending to be asleep or unconscious in A and E to know the difference, and Mimi wasn't making a very good job of it. Soon enough, though, the tension seemed to leave her body and she was really asleep.

Time to go. Rafe tried to come up with some parting words that he might whisper, something to sum up how he felt, but he couldn't. Leaning over, his lips formed the shape of a kiss, which didn't even touch her forehead for fear of waking her. Then, swiftly, he turned away.

* * *

Mimi heard the door close. Despite her jumbled thoughts and the almost irresistible desire to sleep, she knew that Rafe had left now.

He'd looked so tired. Despite that, she knew he would have stayed if she'd asked him, watching over her. But it was time now, and she'd wanted him to get some rest.

Her fingers felt for the watch on her wrist. Still there. The most precious thing he owned…

A great tide of fatigue overwhelmed her. She'd feel better in the morning. The lucky sixpence would see to that.

The watch had stayed on her wrist for the last eight days. It had gone with her from the ICU down to a general ward, and now it was going home with her. Mimi was dressed and sitting by her bed, waiting for Charlie to come and fetch her.

'All set?' He was all smiles when he appeared at the door of the ward.

'Definitely.' She'd been looking at Rafe's watch every five minutes. In addition to the clear message that it carried, it was also useful for telling the time.

'Let's get out of here, then.' Charlie picked up her bag and laid it across his knees. 'Matthew's outside with the car, and Jan's just rustling up a wheelchair for you.'

Mimi winced with embarrassment. 'Sorry. It's all such a business…' Jan and Matthew's house was still drying out and they had given up Charlie's spare bedroom for Mimi. They'd be sleeping at her cottage now, and coming back to Charlie's during the day.

'Oh, be quiet. It's a well-oiled machine, Mimi, so just sit back and watch the cogs go round.'

'I'm beginning to regret giving you such a hard time when you got out of hospital. I can't wait to be able to get around by myself.' Mimi screwed her face up and Charlie laughed.

'You were right.' He leaned forward, doing the mad scientist impression which had always made her laugh when they were kids. 'Now, my pretty, I get my revenge.'

The cool breeze on her face was wonderful. It was as if the world had been waiting for her for the past two weeks and had spruced itself up for her return. The sun shone and the late summer sky was cloudless.

Mimi was installed on the sofa in Charlie's sitting room and Jan bustled off into the kitchen, reappearing with a bouquet in one hand and a parcel in the other. 'These came for you this morning.'

Pink and white roses, with purple freesias for scent. Rafe. He knew she loved freesias.

'I'll get a vase and some water so you can arrange them.' Jan put the flowers down on Mimi's lap and handed her a small white envelope.

She opened it with trembling fingers.

With love from everyone...

No. That wasn't right. Mimi realised her mistake with a stab of regret.

'Who are they from?' Jan was watching her.

'Oh… Everyone I used to work with.' A salt tear reached the stitches on her face and she snatched a tissue from the box on the table and dabbed it gingerly. 'That's so nice of them.'

'They're lovely.' Jan put the package down on

the other end of the sofa and turned towards the kitchen.

Mimi reached for the parcel, trying to work up a bit of enthusiasm for it. Everyone had been so nice over the last couple of weeks, visiting her and sending cards. She'd known that Rafe wouldn't come. It would have only drawn out the sadness of knowing they were inevitably going to part.

But every step she'd made, coming out of the ICU, coming home, had been bittersweet because it was another step towards regaining a life that didn't include Rafe. Mimi shook her head and grabbed the package, taking her frustration out on the tape that secured it.

She almost gave up and left it for Charlie to undo when he came back with the tea. Everything seemed like an effort at the moment. But someone had taken the trouble to wrap it up and send it for her, and the least she could do was to show some interest.

Inside was a pretty patterned box bearing the name of an exclusive skincare company. When she lifted the lid, the fresh scent was gorgeous after the dry, utilitarian smell of the hospital.

Someone had been very thoughtful. Mimi knew she looked a mess; her hair was flat and her nails needed filing and that was just the tip of the iceberg. One leg was in a cast and the other was still swollen, blistered and discoloured from the snake bites. When she'd first been allowed to go to the bathroom at the hospital, the large mirror above the basin had revealed what she'd only glimpsed in the pocket mirror the nurse had given her. Livid bruises on her face, a line of stitches and her own eyes staring back at her in shock and dismay.

She picked up a bar of soap, closed her eyes and smelled it. Her skin itched from antiseptic soap and wipes and this was just what she'd been craving. There were bottles of lotions and shampoo. Mimi picked up a tube of hand cream, squeezing a small dab on to her finger and rubbing it on to the back of her hand, still bruised from where a cannula had been inserted. It was luxurious and smelled just gorgeous.

'Who's that from?' Charlie appeared with a plate of cakes.

'I don't know.' Mimi looked around for a card

but couldn't see one. 'But look, Charlie. So thoughtful…'

'Hmm.' Charlie leaned over to inspect her gift. 'Suppose you'll be wanting to stink my bathroom out with this lot.'

'Oh, stop. You should be so lucky. And if you lay one finger on any of these, you're dead.'

'Hardly likely.' Charlie rummaged around amongst the torn packaging. 'Must be a card somewhere… What's that?' He pointed at a slim package, slipped into the side of the box.

'Don't know.' Mimi tore the tissue paper and caught her breath.

'Very smart.' Charlie peered at the phone in her hand. 'Top of the range. Who's it from, though?'

Suddenly she knew. Mimi pressed the power button on the phone and the screen lit up immediately. There was an unread text.

'How do I…?' She jabbed her finger on the screen and the text appeared.

If there's anything you need, call. Hope you enjoy washing off the smell of the hospital. Love Rafe.

Dumbly, she clasped the phone in both hands, holding it to her heart.

'When did this come, Charlie?'

'Came by courier this morning.'

'It's from Rafe. How did he know I was coming out of hospital today?'

'I've been...' Charlie shrugged. 'I've been keeping him up to date, and asking a few questions about things. You know...texts. Couple of calls.'

From the guilty look on Charlie's face, it had been more than a couple of calls.

Suddenly it was all too much. Mimi felt tears welling in her eyes and she started to cry.

'Hey...sis...' Charlie seemed to manoeuvre almost sideways to get next to the sofa, and slid across to hug her. 'I'm sorry... He said I should call...'

'It's okay. I'm glad you did.' Mimi snuffled into his sweater. 'Is he... Is he all right?'

'He's fine. He was just worried about you and I thought...'

'You thought right. Thank you.' Mimi dabbed at her face with a tissue, wishing that she could at least cry without something hurting. 'Will you call him? Tell him I'm happy to be home, and that I said thank you.'

'Of course.' Charlie hesitated. 'Don't you want to tell him? If he sent you this, then doesn't that mean he wants *you* to call?'

It was tempting, but... 'No. We broke up, and that was the right thing for us both.'

'Yeah. That's what he says. But you know he'll come, don't you? If you want him to.'

'I know. I don't want him to. We don't work that well together, me and Rafe. Never really have done.'

Charlie hugged her tight, rocking her gently in his arms, the way he had the night their parents had died. 'You...loved him, didn't you?'

'Of course I did. Love isn't everything, though. You've got to be able to live with someone.'

'Well, come and live with me. I'll buy your chocolate.'

'You might have to until I get another job.'

Charlie squeezed her hand. 'Don't worry about that, sis. One thing at a time, eh?'

'Yes. One thing at a time.'

She heard the doorbell ring, and Jan's quick footsteps. Then she appeared in the doorway holding another bunch of flowers.

'They're nice.' Charlie turned to look. 'Who are they from?'

'From…' Jan looked at the card which was taped on to the wrappings. 'Joe Harding and everyone at the Old Brewery. Aren't they just lovely?'

'They're beautiful.' Mimi poked Charlie in the ribs. 'Is there anyone you *haven't* told about my coming out of hospital today?'

'Must be someone.' Charlie grinned, sliding back into his wheelchair. 'Right, we'll have tea and then you can get down to some flower arranging. Then a nap…'

'A nap? What? Am I ninety?'

'*Then* you can have a shower.' Charlie nodded towards the box that Rafe had sent and he grinned. 'Then we'll hang out a bit, have some dinner, and tomorrow you can start on the getting well thing. Okay?'

'Okay. Thanks.' Charlie made it sound so easy. They both knew it wasn't, but it paled into insignificance alongside the journey she was going to have to take before she stopped missing Rafe.

It had to be done, though. All of it. Starting tomorrow.

CHAPTER FIFTEEN

MIMI HAD BOUGHT a new dress. She had been exhausted by the shopping trip with Jan, but had refused point-blank to go home until she'd found what she was looking for. A pretty, dusky pink summer dress that she'd got in the sales because everyone was looking forward to the winter fashions now, but which had the advantage of covering her knees.

Tights would have gone some way towards making her leg look a little better, but she still couldn't bear to have anything touch the swollen, discoloured skin around the snake bites. The supportive brace on her other foot didn't do much for the outfit either, but at least it allowed her to walk and she opted for a pink canvas sneaker on the other foot.

She'd applied a deep conditioner to her hair, drying it carefully, and was pleased with the shine it gave. There was nothing she could do to make the scar on her face go away, but a little foundation made it less obvious.

'Bit more cleavage, maybe...' Charlie gave her outfit a cool, assessing eye.

'The neck doesn't go like that. Anyway, what happened to being a woman of mystery?' Mimi pulled at the lace-edged top of the dress.

'There's something you need to learn about men, Mimi. Cleavage is always better than mystery.'

'You think I don't know anything about men?'

Mystery was going to have to do. She had too many imperfections now to consider anything else, and Rafe was going to have to take her as she was. Mimi pulled on her coat and got to her feet.

It had been ten weeks since her accident and, now that the cast was off, it was a lot easier to get around. She couldn't walk very far and still needed elbow crutches to support her, but every day she managed a little more.

Charlie held up his hands in an expression of surrender. 'Not getting involved, Mimi. I'm just giving you a lift.'

'Good. Thanks. Let's get going.'

* * *

Rafe's road was a nice road. Nice houses. If he'd had to spend all this time away from her, Mimi was glad that he'd found somewhere pleasant to live. Charlie drove slowly, pulling up outside the house on the brow of the hill.

'Oh...!'

'Told you.' Charlie looked at the path, sloping upwards with a couple of steps along the length of it, and three more leading to the front door. 'Not all that accessible.'

'Well, what do you do then?'

'I go round the back.' Charlie pointed to the concrete slope where Rafe's car was parked. There was a passageway in between the house and the garage, just wide enough to take a wheel-chair.

It was bad enough turning up at his front door; the back door was out of the question. And if she could get this far, then a few steps weren't going to stand in her way. Even if they did look virtually insurmountable from here.

'Why don't you just call him? That would be much easier.'

As if the rest of this was a walk in the park. 'I'll manage. I'll take it slowly.'

Charlie shrugged. 'Okay. I'll wait.'

'It's okay. Thanks for the lift.' Mimi grabbed her handbag, looping it across her body, and got out of the car, pulling herself upright.

'Call me when you want me to come and get you...'

Charlie waited anyway, while she laboriously made her way up the steep path. The last three steps looked pretty much impossible, but she could reach the bell from the bottom if she stretched up. Turning around, she flapped her hand at Charlie in a signal that he was going now, and the car moved off.

This was it. Charlie had mentioned more than once that there were easier ways of getting to see Rafe, but she'd been determined. It was going to be just her and Rafe. Away from the echoes of their past which haunted her own cottage, and certainly not anywhere else. What she wanted to say needed to be said in private.

She reached for the bell and rang it. No answer. Rafe's car was there and, anyway, Charlie had called to make sure he was in, on the pretext that he might drop round at some point in the morning.

Perhaps he'd gone out for a few minutes, knowing that Charlie would let himself in at the back. Maybe he'd forgotten. Or maybe there was some kind of emergency at the hospital and he'd been called in. But then he would have taken his car.

Mimi tried again, this time keeping her thumb on the bell for long enough to make sure that Rafe was out. Then she carefully made a one-hundred-and-eighty-degree turn and sat down on the front steps.

There was just one cloud in the sky, but it was a big one and it was coming this way. The breeze was fresh and she drew her coat around her, wishing she'd brought her umbrella. It didn't matter now. However long she had to wait, she wasn't going to call Charlie and get him to come back for her.

She waited and then saw him, turning the corner at the end of the road, the Sunday paper tucked under his arm in a thick wad. There were a few moments to appreciate his long stride, the way his dark woollen sweater mimicked the shape of his shoulders. She could just see that he hadn't bothered to shave this morning. She'd always thought that a couple of days' worth of stubble suited Rafe.

She wondered if she should stand up or remain sitting, and decided to stay where she was. The long stretch of front path seemed horribly steep from this angle and she was afraid of falling.

So very afraid of falling. But she was here now, setting herself up for whatever Rafe could dish out. Cold distance, uncertainty, outright rejection. Or the terror of hearing him say *yes.* She'd deal with it when it came. She clasped her hands together tightly, wondering if she'd know when he saw her. Maybe he'd pretend not to for a few strides, to give him time to work out how he was going to let her down easily.

He saw her. The precise moment was clear and unequivocal because he dropped his paper and started to run. When he reached the front path he slowed and suddenly stopped, his gaze on her.

'Mimi. What...?'

'You...you said that if there was anything...' She gulped the words out.

He took the path in long strides, stopping in front of her. 'Come in.'

She swallowed hard, trying to remember the words that she'd rehearsed so many times. Suddenly her courage deserted her. 'I...I can't.'

He sat down next to her on the step, one arm planted on the paving stone behind her, his face a mask of concern. He was being careful not to touch her.

'Okay. We'll stay here, then.'

She wanted this moment to last. Even the tearing uncertainty was something she wanted to hang on to because she was here with him.

'Mimi...?' He craned around to look into her face. 'What is it? Why won't you come inside?'

'Because...' Suddenly it all came tumbling out. 'Because there's something I want you to do for me. I believe in you and I want you to believe in me...'

He opened his mouth to speak and she waved him into silence.

'I believe that we can make it work between us, if we just trust enough to help each other change. I'm daring you to try.'

'You...' He gasped out the word, turmoil showing in his face. 'You're daring me?'

'Yes.' She was twisting her fingers so tightly together that they hurt.

'Then I dare you back, Mimi.' He was closer now, his mouth an inch from hers, his gaze all-encompassing. 'I dare you to come inside.'

'You might be sorry…'

'I won't be. I'll make sure you aren't either.'

'Then I accept.' She held out her hand to shake on the deal, and he pulled her trembling fingers to his lips.

Pulling his keys out of his pocket, he put them into her hand. Then he lifted her in his arms and turned towards the door. In a dream—no, this was far too good to be a dream—Mimi opened the door.

'Last chance, Mimi.' He was smiling down at her. 'If you come inside then you stay until we've seen this one through.'

'I know.'

He stepped over the threshold and the warmth of the house tingled against her cheek. Rafe kicked the door closed and let her down, his arms around her waist, supporting her against his body. She dropped her handbag and slid her coat off her shoulders, letting it fall to the floor.

'Aren't we going to go and sit down?' He wasn't moving, just staring at her.

'I have to do something far more important first.' He held her close, kissing her. Tender at first and then the connection between them snapped into place, something hot and wild flooding through them both.

She'd lived for this. Dreamed of it, every moment that they were apart.

Rafe was showing no sign of wanting to move and she kissed him again. Yesterday was gone and tomorrow wasn't here yet. And today was turning out to be just perfect.

'Maybe we should…talk?'

'Not yet.' He smiled down at her. 'There might be a few constructive arguments along the way…'

'I imagine so. I'm almost hoping there will be.'

'In which case I want to remind us both how sweet it'll be when we make up.'

That sounded like an excellent plan. 'And this is the best you can do?' She knew for sure that it wasn't.

He kissed her again and her legs started to tremble. He felt it and supported her the few steps to the stairs, sitting down before he pulled her on to his lap. 'Better?'

'Much.' She could feel his body against hers. Wound tight, like a coiled spring. 'Rafe, I've missed you so much.'

'Me too...' He grinned. 'I'm not dreaming, am I?'

'If you are, then we're both dreaming together.' Maybe this would shatter the dream. She had to trust him enough to believe it wouldn't.

She swung her feet up, looking at her mismatched footwear. Suddenly her swollen, discoloured leg seemed so much worse than it had looked this morning when she'd got out of bed and her fingers itched to pull her dress down and cover as much of it as she could. But being in his arms gave her courage.

'I feel a mess, and I'm afraid that's all you'll see. I want you to be honest with me...'

'Mimi...' His fingers brushed her cheek, almost finding the healing scar on her face and instinctively she flinched. When his gaze found hers again, tears were glistening in his eyes.

'Mimi, please don't ever feel that you're not the

most beautiful woman in my world. Please don't ever think that I'm judging you.'

'You don't care, do you? About my leg…the scars…' Finally she could manage to say it.

His chest heaved as he sucked in a deep breath. 'I care about them, but only because they hurt you. I love you.'

'And love is blind?'

'Never.' His finger was under her chin, tipping her face up towards his. 'I see every part of you. And I love every part of you. Please don't be afraid, sweetheart, because there's nothing for you to be afraid of.'

'And I…'

He laid his finger over her lips. 'There's more I want to tell you. Your turn in a minute.'

She couldn't help smiling. Rafe was clearly taking this decision to change seriously and it looked as if she was going to have difficulty in shutting him up. 'Okay.'

'I stayed away because it was what we'd agreed, and I thought it was best to let you recover properly without having me around. I wanted to let you make this decision, but I hoped every day that you would.'

'Yes...' It made Mimi feel so good to hear him say these things.

'I want to love you and take care of you, but I want to let you take care of me too.'

'Yes.'

'When you were arguing with me, that night on the sofa when you climbed on top of me...' She felt him shudder.

'That was a mistake. I know.'

He chuckled. 'It was challenging. And, in or out of bed, that's the thing that excites me about you most. I want you to love me, but I *need* you to challenge me, and I need you to make me hear it.' He dropped a kiss on to her cheek.

'Because I'm always right?' She giggled.

'No. Because neither of us is always right. But together we've got a fighting chance.'

'You've been thinking about this, haven't you?'

'All the time. Every day, honey.'

He kissed her again. Rafe had always known all the right things to do to make her body crave him and to make her heart thump with longing for him. An emotion that she couldn't name shivered through her. Desire, happiness. The feeling that she was coming home… No. The knowledge that she *was* home.

This was all she needed. Everything else could take its time.

'Maybe we should take things slowly.' She waited for his agreement.

It didn't come. 'What? Don't you agree, Rafe?'

'What things?'

She dug him in the ribs. 'You know what things. Sex. Leave the gymnastics until later.'

He shrugged. 'Yeah, I can do without the gymnastics. If you honestly want to know, then the sex is going to be a bit harder.' He kissed her cheek. 'I'm not going to pretend that I don't want you. Mimi, I'm done with that. But I'll wait until you're ready, however long that takes.'

He was making this very hard. Mimi wanted him too, but the thought that she might disappoint him held her back. 'I just think… Well, I get tired easily. And my legs are still weak. I can't do all the things we used to.'

'Would it be all right if I just kissed you?'

She looked up into the warmth of his eyes, wondering how she could have lived this long without having him close. 'Yes. It would be more than all right.'

'Hold hands. I'd like to do that.'

She took his hand in hers, kissing his fingers. 'How's that?'

'Wonderful. You want to try something new?'

She grinned. 'What sort of new?'

He kissed her cheek again, working his way round to her ear, and Mimi shivered. 'I'll kiss you and touch you. I'll make you burn for me, the way I do for you, only I'll take it slow. Very slow. Very gentle.'

She could almost feel him doing it. Her fingers clutched convulsively at his sweater. 'Yes. Only you don't need to be all that gentle. I'm not going to break.'

He kissed her, his hands tender and his mouth hot, almost savage. 'Oh, yes, you are, honey. You *are* going to break...'

Rafe had carried her upstairs in a move that seemed romantic rather than a response to need. Mimi sat down on the bed, looking around. Cream walls, cream curtains, cream linen. It was...

It was neat and tidy, but the room could do with some loving care. It felt like a place where you just crashed out to sleep.

'This is…nice.' The bed was large and the mattress comfortable. It was a bit like a high-class hotel room.

He chuckled. 'Needs a woman's touch.'

'Ah. Well, maybe I'll…' Mimi suddenly forgot all about soft furnishings as Rafe pulled his sweater and shirt over his head together in one fluid movement.

'Maybe you'll what?' He knelt down in front of her, gently taking off her shoe and sock.

'I'll touch it later. First I'll touch you.' She ran her fingers lightly over his chest, feeling the muscles quiver and tense. 'I tried so hard to hold you in my imagination, but I couldn't. I was too angry, and you're too beautiful.'

'No more of that now, sweetheart.' He kissed her, smoothing her hair back from her face. 'I want to look at you.'

Suddenly she wanted that too. With all the frailties, the scars, the red blotches on her leg. Even though he was flawless, smooth skin rippling over muscle and bone. 'Help me…with my dress.'

CHAPTER SIXTEEN

HE UNDRESSED HER SLOWLY. Lavished attention on her, trailing his fingers across every inch of her body. When Rafe took his jeans off, she gave him a little gleeful look and he knelt in front of her, holding her close.

'I don't think I ever said this before...' He kissed her lips lightly. 'You make me feel so loved. So wanted.'

'You are loved. You are wanted.' It felt good to say it, and even better to have him hear it.

'I thought...' He seemed to give up any pretence of thought for a moment, in favour of the sweet sensations that his caress, and her answering touch, engendered.

'What did you think?'

'I thought that taking it slow was going to mean a bit of self-restraint. But I want this so much, Mimi. I won't be cheated out of a single moment of it.'

They kissed for a long time. Talking, caressing, both knowing where this was leading and in no hurry to get there. When he finally lifted her on to the bed, Mimi didn't care that he could see all her imperfections, all the injuries that she examined every morning in the mirror. In his eyes, she was beautiful.

'Comfortable?' He put an extra pillow behind her back.

'I'm fine.' She caught hold of his hand, pulling him close, feeling the heat of his skin. 'Where were we?'

The list of things they liked about each other, with a caress and a kiss for each one. He nuzzled against her shoulder, his lips brushing her ear.

'Breasts...' He paused. Hesitation wasn't Rafe's style and he was just letting the thought sink in while his fingers traced across her ribcage. Stopping, just as she began to tremble with anticipation.

'You are such a bad man...'

'Yeah?' His grin confirmed it. 'Is that something you like, or just an observation?'

'Something I like...' She caught her breath as

he ran his tongue across her nipple, lavishing slow attention on it.

They moved past the point of mere arousal to a place where every touch sent sensation spinning through their bodies. Every breath, every word, tangling in a web of pleasure which captured them both.

When the time came, there was no need for Rafe to ask if she was ready. He reached for the condom and handed it to her. Mimi ran one finger down his length, making him groan. Then she rolled the condom down carefully, in an exercise of sensuality triumphing over practicality.

He couldn't believe that this was really happening, but it was much too good to be a dream. Mimi was in his arms, making love with him. More than that, they were at one in a way they'd never been before. Carefully, he propped her leg on to a pillow, then levered his body over hers.

She was staring into his eyes and when he pushed inside her, she murmured his name. Rafe held still for a while, feeling the tremble of his limbs match that of hers. She reached up, her fingers tracing over his face and lips, and he allowed a little of his weight to press down on to her, pouring all his furious need into one kiss.

They were both too greedy for these moments for him to do anything that would snatch them away. He made love to her slowly, luxuriating in her gaze. Every sensation, every emotion shared.

'My beautiful Mimi.' He knew that she was close to breaking point and he wanted her to hear it, and believe it, one more time. When she smiled back at him, he knew that she'd finally learned to accept that compliment completely and that she would accept everything else he had to give.

One hand found his, guiding it to the top of her swollen leg, asking for what she needed silently but without apology. He wrapped his fingers around her thigh, holding her leg steady on the pillow so his movements didn't jolt it.

She felt his other hand curl around her shoulder, steadying her against his thrusts, so she could feel each one more keenly. Mimi raked her nails across his back, feeling him shudder with the sudden sensation, and his rhythm changed. Pushing her further and higher until she came so hard that the earth seemed to tilt.

He held her tight as aftershocks spun through

her body. Keeping her safe, telling her all the things she so needed to hear. How he loved her. That she was beautiful and he was never going to let her go. It was then that Mimi realised that the world hadn't tipped upside down. It had simply righted itself.

Rafe could have just watched her for hours. But then he felt her leg arch around his back, and her fingers touching the place where their bodies were joined.

'Now you…' She didn't really need to tell him; he was already helpless in her hands. She knew he couldn't resist when she did that…

Rafe held on, through each exquisite sensation, until finally it was almost a relief when his shaking limbs began to relax. Knowing they were probably about to turn to jelly, taking his brain along with them, he rolled over to one side of her, pulling her close to feel the beat of her heart against his.

'Wow…' He felt her snuggle in tight as she voiced the only word that was currently available from his own vocabulary.

He kissed the top of her head, feeling his whole body plunge into satiated warmth. 'Mmm. Wow.'

* * *

He fetched a sturdy stool with slip-proof feet, for Mimi to perch on while they showered together. Rafe planted his hands firmly on the tiles behind her shoulders so she could hold on to his arms to steady herself while she soaped him.

'All done.' She ran her fingers through his wet hair, slicking it back from his face.

'You were all done a while ago.' The last ten minutes had been an exercise in sheer pleasure, just for the sake of it.

It was so good to hear her laugh again. So good to feel her limbs tangling with his.

'The last time...' She wrapped her arms around his neck. 'The last time we were in the water together, you carried me out. You saved me, Rafe.'

'I couldn't have made it out of there without you, honey.'

'Can we do it again? Save each other.'

'I'm relying on you, Mimi. I've been lost and I need you to save me.' Warm water tumbled on to his back as he kissed her. It was the sweetest sensation because he knew that he was safe in Mimi's arms.

One hand trailed across his chest and Rafe braced his limbs securely against the side of the shower. He was strong enough to support her, and keep her safe too. Her fingers tantalised, moving lower, and the words she whispered in his ear told him exactly what to expect next. Rafe closed his eyes…

She was tired now. He let her rest for a while, watching her as she slept. More than once, during those silent nights at the hospital, he'd wondered if maybe they shared the same dreams. Now he knew.

When she woke she was hungry and he pulled on his clothes and went downstairs to make tea and toast. When he returned, she was wrapped in his dressing gown, smoothing the creases in her dress.

'Can you stay tonight? I can run you home to get whatever you need, and we'll pick up some shopping. I'll do a Sunday roast, with all the trimmings.' Living on his own, he'd got into the habit of making do with pizza on Sundays and it would be good to cook again.

'Sounds wonderful.' She took the elbow crutch that he'd retrieved from the front step and stood up.

'You want my arm?'

'No, that's okay. Let me manage it on my own.'

He waited while she walked carefully down the stairs, and then fetched the tea from the kitchen. She settled comfortably on to the sofa, leaning against him, and he put his arm around her shoulder.

His heart beat fast and suddenly he couldn't keep the words to himself. 'I want to be with you, Mimi. All the time.'

She flushed red. 'Are you asking me to move in with you?'

'Yeah. Or we can stay at your cottage, if you prefer.'

'Your work's here. And I can't have you doing all that driving...' She broke off, smiling. 'The truth is that I'd rather be here with you, if that's okay. We're going to do things differently from when we were at the cottage.'

'Yeah. I think so too. So you'll come here? Warm my bed at night?'

'Yes, my love, I will.'

Happiness burst into yet another neglected corner of his heart. He took her hand, pulling it to his lips. 'I'm going to make you glad you said that.'

'And I'm going to make you glad you asked.' She grinned impishly. 'Maybe…'

Rafe leaned back against the sofa cushions, chuckling. 'All right. What have I let myself in for now?'

'Well, there are a few little bits and pieces I could bring with me. Only if you wanted me to. My breadmaker, perhaps.'

'Bring as much as you like.' Rafe looked round at the sitting room. Plain walls. Good quality furniture. But it had always felt a little cold and empty. He'd known for a while now that there was one vital thing missing. 'I said that this place needed a woman's touch. What I actually meant was that it needs *your* touch.'

'Really?'

'Absolutely. There's a bit of a space, up in the bedroom. I think it needs something…'

'A washstand?'

Rafe laughed. 'Perfect.'

'I've got some other things up in the loft. Things

we bought together. You could go up there and have a look around if you wanted.'

'You didn't throw it all away?'

'No. I couldn't bear to. I just didn't want to look at it.' She shifted in his arms and settled again comfortably. 'Maybe this is how we do it. Keep the things we want, but make a new start.'

'I'd like that.'

They were silent for a moment. Dreaming the same dreams.

'What are you thinking, Rafe?'

Rafe bent to kiss her. 'I was just thinking about coming home every day to find you in my bed. Naked. Or maybe something lacy...'

'You will not.' She poked her tongue out at him. 'That's only every other day. Alternate days, you're the one who gets naked. In the kitchen.'

He chuckled. 'Right. Okay, I see how this is going to go...'

'And there are rules.' She pulled herself up on to his lap and he curled his arms around her.

'Yeah. I was really hoping for rules.'

She'd never felt so loved before. Never felt that she was so exactly in the right place.

'Rule Number One...' Mimi kissed the tip of his finger. 'We talk about it. Whatever it is, however hard it is.'

'Agreed. That's a good one. Number Two...' He laughed as she kissed his next finger. 'You remember that I love you. And if I ever do anything to make you feel you're not good enough, you make me crawl on my hands and knees to ask for forgiveness.'

'I think you're pretty safe on that score. But yes, I can do that.'

'Good. Number Three...'

'Hey, don't I get to make the next one?'

'Do you have one?'

She thought for a moment. 'No. Not at the moment. Okay, you take Three and I'll have Number Four.'

'Fair enough. Number Three is that we don't let the sun go down on an argument.'

'Yes, that's a good one. That can be Number Three.' She kissed the top of his third finger. 'Where did you get that one from?'

'Remember the old guy we went to see?' He frowned in thought for a moment. 'Infected cut on his leg. What was his name?'

'Toby? His name's not really Toby, but his surname is Jugg, so everyone in the village calls him Toby.'

Rafe chuckled. 'Okay, well, the wise Mr Jugg suggested it to me.'

'When did he do that?'

'When you were off fetching the dressings and conspiring with his next-door neighbour. He gave me some relationship advice.'

'I wasn't gone *that* long, was I?'

'It was a pretty one-sided conversation and he came directly to the point. Toby seemed to think that the fact I was looking at you when you weren't looking, and looking away when you were, was a sign that I was madly in love with you. He was quite right, of course, and naturally I denied it all.'

'It's a good rule. Did he happen to mention anything else that might come in handy?'

A faint gleam appeared in Rafe's eyes. 'That was man-to-man advice. Don't interfere.'

'Okay. Rule Number Four is that I'm going get it out of you.' She kissed the sensitive skin on his neck.

'Yeah, I imagine you will. Soon, probably.'

* * *

Step by step, she was moving back into the world. Rafe had talked to the HR department where he worked, and it had been arranged that Mimi should go in four half-days a week to mentor trainee ambulance technicians. It was unpaid, but it was a start. And, to her surprise, she found that she loved teaching just as much as she loved being on the road. It was one more new possibility in a world that felt full of promise.

Although the snake bites were still painful and she was unable to put her full weight on that leg, her other leg was strong enough to make walking easier. And although the scar on her face was still there, it was no longer the only thing that Mimi saw when she looked in the mirror.

When the invitation to the grand reopening of the Old Brewery came, Rafe had voiced his concerns that it might awaken traumatic memories for her. But when Mimi had told him that with him by her side she could take that risk, he'd simply hugged her and promised his support. With his trust, she felt she could do almost anything.

The afternoon was bright and clear. The colours of the autumn leaves were especially vibrant this year, deep reds and oranges lining the road, and, as they turned into the car park of the Old Brewery, Joe Harding came to meet them.

'So glad you could come.' He offered Mimi his arm, helping her out of the car. 'This way.'

He led them through to the visitor centre, which had been cleared and hung with bunting for the party. A barbecue had been set up in the beer garden behind the building and there were several different kinds of beer on tap.

Grant made a point of bringing his wife and children over and introducing them, and then Joe Harding made a speech, which was received with general approval, in particular because it was short and to the point. A little girl dressed as a fairy appeared from somewhere and everyone clapped as she presented Mimi with a posy of flowers. Rafe seemed so happy that he was almost shining. And then Charlie turned up.

'Who's that?' She turned to Rafe, tugging urgently at his sleeve.

'Um…one of the nurses from the ICU, I think.'

'Really? You mean I was lying unconscious and Charlie was busy chatting up the ICU nurses?'

Rafe nodded, grinning. 'Looks like it.'

'Good for him. She's pretty, isn't she?'

'Not as pretty as you...' He leaned down to whisper the words and then grunted in protest as Mimi jabbed him in the ribs.

'It's not a competition, you know. Aren't you glad that Charlie's found someone nice?'

'Of course. Think he'll introduce us any time soon?'

'He'd better...' Charlie seemed to finally realise that Mimi was staring at him and she gave him a wave. 'Go and ask them if they're free for lunch tomorrow.'

'Ask them yourself. They're coming over.' Rafe turned his smile on to the petite brunette who was with Charlie.

It had been a lovely afternoon. Fireworks were promised for the evening, and Mimi and Rafe had escaped the heat of the visitor centre for a while.

'Ah! It's better out here.' She had left her elbow crutches behind, in favour of leaning on his arm. 'Fewer people around.' She turned and kissed him.

'What's that for?'

'To thank you for today. And to remind you that I might want to thank you a bit more comprehensively when we get home.'

Rafe chuckled. 'You know what, I'm sending you back to work full-time. Four half-days a week isn't enough to keep your mind occupied.'

'You love it. Anyway, if you want me to stop thinking about sex, then you'd better stop with the *How many ways can we do this without my leg swelling?* thing.'

'That's Continuous Professional Development. Not every doctor has his very own adder bite patient to experiment on, you know.'

'So that's what you call it, is it? What happens when I get better?'

'I experiment a bit more. Long-term effects.'

They walked a few steps in the darkness and Rafe found a bench. It was obviously designed for visitors to watch the comings and goings at the working brewery because it looked out over the river and across to the floodlit loading bay.

'Do you want to go down there?' His voice was very tender. 'Joe Harding lent me the key.'

'You know...' Mimi thought for a moment,

wondering if she really did or she really didn't, and decided that she did. 'Yes. Yes, I would.'

He fetched her coat, wrapping it around her, and carried her across the rough ground between the visitor centre and the loading bay. It wasn't strictly necessary, she probably would have managed it on her own, but she needed him close.

'I'd like to go inside.' She could feel herself trembling, but she wanted to do this. She'd shared everything else with Rafe over the last weeks, and both of them had known that she'd share this sooner or later.

He bent down, unlocking the padlock and pulling the shutter up from the door beside the main bay. Reaching inside, he found the light switch.

'Sure about this?'

'Yeah.'

He wound his arm around her waist, helping her inside. Everything was clean and orderly, and the smell of the brewing beer was stronger here now than it had been the last time. She looked around. The stairs where Rafe had been standing. The metal door which had flown off the wall. The shuttered entrance that she'd made a dash for before the door had hit her and the water had swept her off her feet.

She'd dreamed of this place, waking up in the night to find him holding her, comforting her. And, now she was here, it had somehow lost its power. Something bad had happened here, but that was all in the past.

He helped her across to a bench, which stood against the wall, and she sat down on his lap. When she looked up into his face, she saw tears in his eyes.

'Hey… We made it, Rafe.'

'Yeah. We did. Are you okay?'

Funnily enough, yes. Mimi hadn't expected to be, but then she imagined that Rafe hadn't expected not to be.

'Yes. You're not, though, are you?'

He smiled. 'Just being here…I thought I'd lost you. When you were under the water and I was searching for you…'

She kissed his cheek. 'And you found me. That's what matters, Rafe.'

'Yeah. I know.'

She hadn't expected that this would be the time

or the place, but it was. Mimi reached into her handbag.

'I have something for you.'

He brushed his hand across his face. 'Yeah? What?'

'Your watch. I know you said you wanted me to keep it...'

She pulled the jeweller's box out of her bag and gave it to him. Rafe shot her a questioning look and opened it.

'Mimi...' His face broke into a wide grin. 'That's... It's great.'

'You don't mind?'

'Mind? It's wonderful.' There were two watches in the box—Rafe's along with a smaller one for her, each with half the lucky sixpence mounted behind the hands.

'Put it on...' She could hardly sit still, hardly wait to see it on his wrist.

'Yours first.' He slid the bracelet of the smaller watch over her hand, fixing the clip to secure it tight. Then he took off the watch he'd been wearing for the last couple of months and let her put his grandfather's watch back on to his wrist.

'I had to have the dial redone.' She traced her

finger over the glass. After some debate, she'd opted for a dark blue semi-circle, studded with stars, to replace the other half of the sixpence. 'It's a reminder of the nights you sat with me. How much that meant to me.'

'It's perfect, honey. I love it, thank you.' He stared at the watch for long moments and Mimi hugged herself with glee. She hadn't dared hope that he'd like it as much as he obviously did.

'I've got something for you too.' He reached into the inside pocket of his jacket. 'I was going to save it for later, but you're right. This is the place.'

He was hiding something in his hand and, when curiosity got the better of her and she leaned over to see what it was, he smiled.

'Are you ready?'

'I might be, if I knew...' Mimi caught her breath. Suddenly she *did* know.

She gazed up into his eyes and he nodded, as if the question was already asked and answered.

'Will you marry me, Mimi?'

'Yes, Rafe. I will.' She didn't need to think about it. Something had clicked into place as soon as he'd spoken the words, a final, all-engulfing happiness which knew no half measures and allowed no hesitation.

'You sound pretty sure of it.'

'I am. I love you, Rafe, and I want to marry you.'

'Then the sooner I can get this on to your finger...' He opened his hand, showing her a box with a ring inside. A pretty, twisting trail of sapphires with a large diamond in the middle. Suddenly it all became real, and tears sprang into her eyes.

'How long...?'

'I chose it last week, but the jeweller had to resize it. I picked it up when I went to town this morning, reckoning I'd give it to you tonight... Do you like it?'

'It's gorgeous, Rafe. Beautiful... Too much...'

He shot her a reproving look. 'Nothing's too much for you, Mimi. I just want to see you wearing it.'

'I...I really want to wear it too.' She held out her hand.

He kissed her finger and then slid the ring on to it. Mimi stared at it. 'Am I dreaming?'

'If you are, then so am I. For the rest of my life.'

* * *

You find a girl you like and...you lead her up the hill to the church...

Toby Jugg's advice. In a moment, Rafe would tell her that this was Rule Number Four, the one he'd set for himself that day when Mimi had appeared on his doorstep. But, for now, he was complete in a way that he'd never thought possible. He'd carry her out of here one more time and give her a moment to show Charlie her ring. And then he'd take her home.

EPILOGUE

IT WAS THE first wedding of the New Year. Charlie had decided to wait at the church, to accompany Mimi down the aisle and give her away, and she snuggled into the horse-drawn carriage with Jack and his daughter, Ellie.

'Are you warm enough, sweetie?' Mimi's wedding dress had a matching brocade coat, with white fur at the collar and cuffs, and Ellie had a similar coat over her dress.

'Yes.' The little girl was trying very hard to be grown up, and to act like a princess, after her father had told her that this was really a fairytale carriage.

'That's good.' Mimi twitched a rug over Ellie's lap, covering her satin slippers. 'Look at the people, coming to watch. You can wave if you like.'

A small knot of people had tumbled out of the village Post Office and were waving to the carriage as it went by. Ellie scrambled up onto her knees on the seat, waving back, almost dropping her posy of flowers out of the window, before Jack retrieved it and stowed it carefully under the seat.

She felt for the heavy pearls around her neck, making sure that they were still there. Rafe's mother had given them to her, saying that her own mother had worn them on her wedding day. Rafe had stopped Mimi from protesting that she couldn't possibly take such a precious gift, and his mother had beamed with pleasure when she saw that they complemented her dress perfectly.

'Are you all right?' Jack must have asked the question at least twenty times, but it still seemed to require an answer.

'I'm fine. Just thinking about…everything. A lot's happened in the last few months, for both of us.'

'Yes.' Jack looked out of the window. 'Might be more to come. You and Rafe can think about me battling through three feet of snow, while you're off on your honeymoon.'

'I'll do no such thing. I'll be…' Mimi laughed as Jack's hands moved for Ellie's ears.

'Okay. We all know what you'll be doing.'

'What will she be doing?' Ellie climbed onto her father's knee, and Jack rolled his eyes.

'Exercises, sweetheart. Mimi has to exercise her leg for a while longer, so that she can walk properly.'

It had been a long, hard journey to get here. The snake bites had weakened Mimi's leg to such an extent that at one point it was doubtful whether she'd be able to make it up the aisle unaided. Rafe had been quite prepared to carry her, saying that he didn't care how she got there, just as long as she did, but Mimi had been determined not to compromise either the date of her wedding, or the manner in which she arrived.

As they pulled up at the church it started snowing again. Large umbrellas shielded her as Jack helped her down from the carriage, and then he stepped back so she could join Charlie in the vestibule of the country church.

There was a moment's pause while Ellie was coaxed to stand a few feet in front of her, ready to scatter petals. Charlie suddenly caught her hand.

'Can you do it on your own?'

'Yes. I can do it.' She wasn't going to stumble,

now. She knew exactly where she was going, and falling flat on her face was no longer an option.

Charlie nodded. 'Off you go, then.'

'But Charlie…? You're supposed to be walking me down the aisle?'

'Yeah. Since when did we care what we were supposed to do? *I* want to see you do this by yourself.' Charlie pressed her hand to his lips in a gesture of old-fashioned charm. 'Go to him, Mimi. I'll be right behind you.'

'I love you, Charlie.'

'Love you too. Just get on with it, will you.'

Mimi turned to face the congregation. Everyone's face was tipped round, towards her. All their friends and family. There would be time for all of them later, but right now all she could see was Rafe.

He looked so handsome in his dark suit and brocade waistcoat, the subtle pattern of which matched the theme of her dress. The organist struck up the Wedding March, and the sudden wall of sound made Ellie jump and run back towards Mimi, instead of walking up the aisle, scattering petals as she was supposed to.

Charlie caught Ellie, lifting her up onto his lap,

and she decided that now was a good time to start throwing petals. Rafe was chuckling, holding out his hand towards her. Mimi couldn't wait any longer. Leaving Charlie to follow with Ellie, she almost ran up the aisle towards him.

* * * * *

Look out for the next great story in the
STRANDED IN HIS ARMS *duet*

SAVED BY THE SINGLE DAD

And if you enjoyed this story, check out these other great reads from Annie Claydon

DISCOVERING DR RILEY
THE DOCTOR SHE'D NEVER FORGET
DARING TO DATE HER EX
SNOWBOUND WITH THE SURGEON

All available now!

MILLS & BOON®
Large Print Medical

April

Waking Up to Dr Gorgeous	Emily Forbes
Swept Away by the Seductive Stranger	Amy Andrews
One Kiss in Tokyo...	Scarlet Wilson
The Courage to Love Her Army Doc	Karin Baine
Reawakened by the Surgeon's Touch	Jennifer Taylor
Second Chance with Lord Branscombe	Joanna Neil

May

The Nurse's Christmas Gift	Tina Beckett
The Midwife's Pregnancy Miracle	Kate Hardy
Their First Family Christmas	Alison Roberts
The Nightshift Before Christmas	Annie O'Neil
It Started at Christmas...	Janice Lynn
Unwrapped by the Duke	Amy Ruttan

June

White Christmas for the Single Mum	Susanne Hampton
A Royal Baby for Christmas	Scarlet Wilson
Playboy on Her Christmas List	Carol Marinelli
The Army Doc's Baby Bombshell	Sue MacKay
The Doctor's Sleigh Bell Proposal	Susan Carlisle
Christmas with the Single Dad	Louisa Heaton